Every night before Abbey went to sleep she would stand at the window in her front room, looking over at Joshua's house, at the twinkle of fairy lights still strung beautifully around the front.

It looked as though another world was just beyond those eaves—another world where Joshua and his children lived…children who had become as much a part of her heart as their father.

Abbey would blow three kisses towards the house, one for each occupant, and then she'd head to her bedroom, lying beneath the ceiling fan, dreaming of a time when she might also be included in the gorgeous family who made her feel so incredibly happy.

She loved Joshua, she loved the twins, and she so desperately wanted to be a part of their life.

Would they let her merge? Let their lives intermingle? She knew the twins wouldn't mind, but would Joshua? Would he be able to trust himself enough to enter into the world of marriage once more?

Lucy Clark is a husband-and-wife writing team. They enjoy taking holidays with their two children, during which they discuss and develop new ideas for their books using the fantastic Australian scenery. They use their daily walks to talk over characterisation and fine details of the wonderful stories they produce, and are avid movie buffs. They live on the edge of a popular wine district in South Australia, and enjoy spending family time together at weekends.

Recent titles by the same author:

A BABY FOR THE FLYING DOCTOR
A BABY TO CARE FOR
NEW BOSS, NEW-YEAR BRIDE
BRIDE ON THE CHILDREN'S WARD

THE DOCTOR'S DOUBLE TROUBLE

BY
LUCY CLARK

First published in Great Britain 2010
Large Print edition 2011
Harlequin Mills & Boon Limited,
Eton House, 18-24 Paradise Road,
Richmond, Surrey TW9 1SR

© Anne and Peter Clark 2010

ISBN: 978 0 263 21721 6

Printed and bound in Great Britain
by CPI Antony Rowe, Chippenham, Wiltshire

THE DOCTOR'S DOUBLE TROUBLE

For Peter K—redeemed at last!
Ps 19:14

CHAPTER ONE

FOR one brief moment, Abigail Bateman wasn't at all sure she'd made the right decision. She'd joined Pacific Medical Aid because she'd needed a change. A change of scenery, a change of pace and a change in her life. Yet as she looked around at the blend of reds, greens and oranges of the outback, she wondered if she hadn't made a huge mistake.

PMA was a good company; she had many friends who worked for them and she'd thought it had been an answer to her prayers. It was an organisation that provided medical support to various countries around the world but also to the outback of Australia, where medical support was difficult to come by.

However, until now she had failed to fully comprehend that she would literally be stuck out in the middle of nowhere. As the small Cessna had circled over the township of Yawonnadeere Creek in the northern part of South Australia, Abbey had felt a tightening in her stomach. Had she done the right thing?

She was travelling alone, just the pilot and herself, and as the wheels of the plane touched the ochre dirt beneath them, she let out the breath she hadn't realised she'd been holding.

'Told ya you'd be fine,' the dark-skinned pilot said, his white teeth straight and bright as he laughed at her anxiety. 'You was flying with the best, Doc. Besides that, Josh would have pounded me one if I'd have let anythin' happen to ya. Yawonnadeere needs another doc and you're it, dearie.'

He brought the small plane to a stop but Abbey didn't move, mainly because she had no idea how to open the door. What had the pilot said his name was? Marden? Morgan? Now her mounting anxiety was starting to affect her memory!

She was too busy trying to take in the expanse of the sparse landscape.

A few hardy Australian bushes and gumtrees were littered here and there, their green leaves stark in contrast to the reddish-brown dirt. Over to her left was a large tin shed, which she presumed was the hangar or airport lounge. Ah… somewhere cool. At least, she hoped it was cool in there.

She smiled at the thought and started to feel a little better as her pilot opened the door, helping her to alight from the aircraft. Being alone at times like these, times of apprehension and concern, was something she'd learned to avoid because her mind often took her to a place where she ended up in tears. Controlling her emotions was far easier when she was working. Being in control was vitally important to her. Even more so in the past three years, ever since her life had come crashing down in a crumbling mess around her feet. Rebuilding was never easy but she knew for a fact that she was stronger now than she'd been before the diagnos— Well, now was hardly the time to think about the past.

She stood on the airstrip and looked around, while her pilot reached into the cargo hold for her luggage. Two suitcases. That's all she'd brought with her to survive the next six months out here in the middle of nowhere. When she'd originally signed with PMA, she'd wanted to get out there into the big wide world, helping others, making a difference rather than focusing on her own problems. She'd expected to go overseas, to a developing country, but when they'd told her she'd be heading to the outback, that there was just as big a need for doctors to work in her own country as there were overseas, she'd begun to wonder if she'd made the right decision.

'Too late now,' she murmured to herself, and was surprised when a rich, deep chuckle of laughter sounded from behind her.

'You've got that right, Doctor.'

Abbey turned around, her jaw almost dropping to the dirt as she came face to face with the last person she'd ever expected to see again. Tall, about six feet four, he had short brown hair hidden beneath a bush hat. Blue eyes naked to the sun and a mouth curved in derision, it could be none other than her medical-school nemesis.

'Joshua Ackles?' Great. He was the last person she needed right now.

'Abigail?'

Both of them were momentarily stunned but as they stood there Abbey could feel the tension building in her neck.

'I only got told a Dr A. Bateman was coming.' Joshua was the first to recover, trying to ignore the way his gut tightened at the sight of her petite frame. But he knew of old not to underestimate her. Abigail Bateman had been a thorn in his side for the last two years of medical school. They'd had most of their classes together and had often vied for the top spot. That was when the rivalry between them had started. Although, he had to admit, their rivalry had helped him to reject any appreciation of her prettiness. Back then, she'd had long, rich, chocolaty-brown hair, which he'd often wanted to touch, to sift his fingers through the silky strands. Then she'd had those big expressive brown eyes, which had been able to twist his gut in both pain and pleasure at the same time. He leaned against the plane and crossed his arms over his chest, noting to his annoyance that she was still very pretty indeed. 'So I take it you actually passed medical school.'

His words helped to break the stunned-fish look that she was sure was on her face, her earlier apprehension at her new adventure rising as she removed her sunglasses and glared at him. 'Oh, that is just so typical of you.'

'Here ya go, Doc,' the pilot said, putting her two suitcases beside her. 'G'day, Josh.'

'Morgan.' Joshua nodded a greeting to his mate but didn't take his eyes off Abbey. 'And what do you mean, that's just so typical of me?'

Abbey spread her arms wide, swatting flies as she did so. 'It's been, what, sixteen years since med school, Joshua, and this is how you react?'

'How *I* react?' He waved a fly away.

'The first thing you say to me is negative. One would hope that after so many years you would have acquired a sense of decorum. Obviously not.'

'Decorum?' He ground the word between his teeth, clenching his hands at his sides in order to stop himself from following through on the child-ish wish of knocking her brand-spanking-new, wide-brimmed hat from her pretty little head.

Morgan laughed at both of them. 'You two sound like my kiddies.'

'See?' Abbey pointed out, before putting her sunglasses back on, steadying her shoulder bag and hefting up her two suitcases, one in each hand. 'I presume this is the way to town?' She didn't wait for an answer but headed towards the tin shed. 'Thank you for a safe flight, Morgan,' she called over her shoulder, determined that the sight of Joshua Ackles wouldn't let her forget her manners.

How was it at all possible that a man she hadn't

seen for sixteen years could rile her within seconds of meeting again? It was ridiculous. The last time she'd seen Joshua had been when they'd come out of their final medical exams, exams that they had both hoped would get them the points they needed to get into their chosen specialities.

They'd had nearly all of their classes together and had even been lab partners for one term. That had been like a volatile roller-coaster, but at least they had both been committed to working hard and achieving an excellent result. Unfortunately, that had also been the term when two of their close friends had started dating, which meant they'd not only had to put up with each other during the day but go out with their friends at the weekend. Still, Abbey had hoped that the passing of sixteen years might have tamed his arrogance. Apparently she was wrong.

'You're still as stubborn as ever,' he growled as he came up beside her, wrenching first one then the other suitcase from her grasp. 'Jeepers. What did you pack in here? The kitchen sink?'

Abbey's eyes widened in annoyance and she tried to grab her luggage back from him but he was far stronger and much faster than her. 'What business is it of yours what I packed? I'm here for six months and I had no idea what I might need.'

'So you packed everything? Water may be scarce out here, Abigail, but we do have a fairly adequate supply. You didn't need to bring your own.'

Abbey fumed. Morgan chuckled and Joshua disappeared into the tin shed before she could say another word, her suitcases disappearing with him. Miserably, Abbey trailed after him.

'You guys know each other?' Morgan asked.

'We went to the same medical school,' Abbey supplied.

'We were fierce competitors, both wanting the top mark,' Joshua added, and nodded. 'It was good. Forced me to work harder.'

Abbey stopped and stared at him for a moment, confusion marring her features. It was the last thing she would have expected him to admit. While Joshua had most certainly bugged her to the point where she'd wanted to deck him, the way they'd fed off each other, the need to outdo each other had provided her own motivation for working harder.

'I never did find out your final score,' he continued as he walked out of the opposite door of the shed from the one they'd come in through, her suitcases still firmly in his grasp.

'Whatever it was, I'm sure it was higher than yours.'

'You didn't attend graduation,' he pointed out.

'My father died,' she returned, as calm as a cucumber, hoping the news would make him feel bad for even mentioning it.

He stopped then and turned to look at her. 'Oh, Abigail. I'm sorry. I didn't know.' His words were deep and heart-felt and for some strange reason his sympathy made her eyes well with tears. It was ridiculous. Her father had died years ago and while she still missed him, she'd come to terms with his death. To feel this way, to have Joshua's words mean so much to her, made her incredibly uncomfortable.

'Well, it was a long time ago,' she remarked, unable to look at him. She started walking again, heading through the shed and back out into the late morning sunshine. Even though it was just after eleven o'clock in the morning, out here in Yawonnadeere the sun was well and truly up. The flies were all around them, buzzing and being a general nuisance. There were insect sounds coming from the surrounding bushes and a kookaburra sitting in a gum tree laughing at her. It was completely different from the hustle and bustle of Sydney, where she'd been this time yesterday.

Last night, after flying to Adelaide and staying in a hotel close to the airport, she'd been slightly apprehensive about what she'd find in her new place of residence. She knew in her heart of hearts that joining PMA had been the right thing to do. Helping people was what she had to do, using her medical skills in a more prominent way rather than just being another faceless doctor in a large city hospital. Cancer had a way of making you re-evaluate your life and that was how Abbey felt it best to deal with her own. She'd expected the next six months to be different, she'd expected the next six months to be a big adjustment, but what she hadn't expected was to be joined at the hip with Joshua Ackles!

'How long have you been here?' she asked after they'd been walking for a few minutes. From the air, the town hadn't seemed that far away from the airstrip but as there were no cars in sight, it appeared she was going to have to walk. It also sank in that as the other doctor in town, Joshua was her only welcoming committee.

'In Yawonnadeere?'

'No, standing on this stretch of dirt path,' she muttered sarcastically, but he heard.

'I see that sarcasm of yours is still in full swing.'

'Perhaps it's a form of protection?'

He stopped under a patch of shade provided by an overhanging gumtree, putting her suitcases down. How had this woman managed to get firmly back beneath his skin in such a very short time? He felt the old hackles rising and turned to face her. 'Protection? From what?'

'From people asking me stupid questions.' She pulled her sunglasses off in order to pierce him with her stare. 'From people making me feel as though I'm back in school when in reality I'm a full-grown woman, coming to an outback community to help people who need it.' Her voice had risen as she'd spoken and she'd stepped closer to Joshua, almost coming up into his face. The fact that she was only five feet four made it difficult to actually intimidate him but she'd done it before and she could do it again. 'You always brought out the worst in me. I hate that.' Her voice was still loud and abrasive.

'You always brought out the worst in *me*,' he countered, shifting so that he was looking down directly into *her* face. 'And *I* hate it, too.'

'You're not allowed to hate it. I'm the newcomer here. I'm hot. I'm tired. I have no idea where I really am or what I'm supposed to be doing for the next six months. I've been through a terrible couple of years and now, when I come into town, completely out of my comfort zone, I'm confronted with *you*.' Abbey came even closer, poking Joshua in the chest. 'Back off, buddy, cos I don't need this.'

'Neither do I. You think you're the only one in the world that's had a tough couple of years? Get in line, honey. The world didn't revolve around you back in medical school and it doesn't revolve around you now.' Joshua's words were vehement and it was only after he'd finished speaking that he realised just how close he was to Abigail, his chest almost knocking her hat from her head.

He looked down into her upturned face, her brown eyes wide with exasperation, her lips together in a firm line, hands planted firmly on her hips. She was a pint-sized dynamo and while she had thoroughly wound him up in the past, he'd always felt a veiled thread of admiration for her.

The fact that she was as beautiful now, with her hat pulled down covering her rich brown locks, as she'd been back in medical school was exactly what he'd expected. The heat, the anger, the pulse that was thundering through both of them now started to change. Josh felt it, the awareness, the powerful animalistic attraction that had simmered between them right through final year. Back then they'd been young enough and dedicated enough to their studies to ignore it, even though they'd perhaps, unknowingly, used it to spur each other on.

Now, they were both adults who were no longer competing for first place. Instead, they were standing beneath the shade of a coolabah tree, in the middle of a dirt track somewhere in the northern part of South Australia, allowing past emotions to overwhelm them. It was utterly ridiculous to allow Joshua Ackles to rile her the way he had all those years ago. She'd just turned forty and was astounded that in the sixteen years since she'd seen him, he was exactly the same.

Exactly. Right down to the way the muscles in his neck seemed to strain and tense whenever she was around. It wasn't the first time they'd yelled at each other and she supposed it wouldn't be the last. What she hadn't expected was the way her body seemed to be reacting to his nearness. He was all but standing over her, glaring down at her with those ice-blue eyes of his, blue eyes that had haunted her back in their final year. The fact that there had been repressed feelings between them was something she was now beginning to understand. Opposites had been known to attract before and she knew that while he'd always infuriated her to the nth degree, she also knew that if he'd kissed her, she wouldn't have slapped his face for taking such liberties.

Would she slap his face now? Abbey swallowed,

her anger starting to dissipate as her gaze flicked to encompass his firm mouth. His face was still all hard angles, gorgeous to the point where she wanted to caress it, to feel the roughness of the morning growth of whiskers tingle the tips of her fingers, to touch him…just as she'd wanted to all those years ago.

She swallowed again, this time her lips parting as she allowed the pent-up air to escape. They were both angry, just as they had been all those years ago when they'd come out of the final exam.

They'd sat at opposite sides of the exam hall, they'd walked out different doors, they'd stood on opposite sides of the steps of the old building, their gazes locking across the crowd of students between them. Abbey had squared her shoulders and lifted her head proudly, letting him know she was certain she'd beaten him. Joshua had raised his chin, piercing her with one of his steel-blue looks before turning away, letting her know he didn't really care what her score was because he was certain he'd done better.

Years later, it appeared they were still squaring off against each other but whereas back then they'd perhaps not even acknowledged the depth of their true emotions, as adults it was hard not to realise what was really buzzing between them... and it wasn't the flies.

Joshua swallowed, his Adam's apple working up and down his throat, drawing her gaze down for a second before she met his eyes once more. The fact that he was looking at her lips, that he was licking his own, made her wonder exactly what *was* happening between them. Adult or not, this still wasn't what she wanted. To reluctantly acknowledge she found him attractive was one thing, but to stand there looking up at him, so close that his sweaty, earthy scent wound itself around her, deepening the need she felt to touch him...that was definitely something else.

Anger disappearing, only to be replaced by awareness, was wrong. He wanted the anger back, to keep Abigail at a very long arm's length. He didn't want someone from his past infringing on the future he'd struggled to build for himself and his children, yet here she was, standing toe to toe with him, giving as good as she got, as she always had. The anger may have gone, the realisation that he'd always been attracted to her may have come, but getting involved with her on a personal level in any way, shape or form was completely out of the question.

Colleagues. She was here for the next six months and to say he could do without her medical assistance would be an outright lie. Medical help was needed and PMA had sent her. He wished, though, that he'd asked for a more detailed dossier on his new locum because at least that way he could have been better prepared when he'd first seen her.

His mind started to clear even more and he forced himself to look away from the plump, red lips that were enticing him. No doubt if he'd followed through on his impulse to clamp his mouth firmly over Abigail's, the only flavour he would have tasted would have been smug female. If he'd given in to the impulse, surely she would have used it to her advantage, pointing out in that haughty manner of hers just what a Neanderthal he was and always had been.

Joshua sucked in a breath and gave her sweet and luscious-looking lips one last glance before pulling superhuman strength from somewhere and taking two steps away, nonchalantly swatting at the flies around them.

'Best get you out of this heat, given you're not used to it.' With that, he turned, picked up her suitcases and started walking.

Abbey was stunned, to say the least. What had just happened? They'd both slipped back into their childish habit of arguing and then they'd become overwhelmingly aware of each other and now he was just…going. She knew she had to follow, that she had no idea where she was or where she was headed, but just for a moment she stood there and watched him walk away.

He seemed taller than she recalled but it was no doubt her mind playing tricks on her. After all, his back was the same and she'd watched him turn and walk away from her enough times to know! But his shoulders were definitely broader, firmer and with more muscle. Perhaps they only appeared to be bigger, given that he was wearing a dark blue T-shirt instead of the crisp white shirt he'd worn throughout medical school. His legs were just as long as she remembered and again, with the addition of shorts rather than jeans or trousers, he looked more rugged, more toned, more handsome than ever before.

Sighing, Abbey hefted her shoulder bag more firmly into position, pushed her hat down harder and swatted at a few more flies. The instant she stepped from the shade, she felt the heat hit her and she really wanted to know why there wasn't a car around to drive her to wherever it was she needed to be.

She'd tried to do some research on the small township of Yawonnadeere Creek. Most of the people who lived there worked in the LPG gas rig situated twenty kilometres away. The town had one full-time police officer, one vet and two full-time doctors. Only, as she'd been informed by her PMA contact, the old female doctor who'd been in the town for well over fifty years had recently passed away, hence the need for a replacement. Since doctors, especially those with experience in emergency medicine, rarely ventured into the outback of Australia, PMA had organised for locums to provide medical care on a six-month rotation. Abbey was, therefore, contracted for six months to be here in the middle of nowhere, with the dirt and the flies and the annoying Joshua Ackles.

The land was by no means flat, as she'd expected it to be. Instead, it was peppered with little hills here and there and as she trudged up a small hill, feeling as insignificant as an ant in this vast area, she saw, laid about below them, the township of Yawonnadeere Creek.

'Wow.'

Joshua was about a metre in front of her and

he paused for a moment to turn back and look at Abigail standing there looking down at the place he called home. She had a look of happiness and wonderment, mixed with a little awe. Did she really like it or was she just trying to be polite? Her hat and sunglasses shielded her eyes but as she stood there, pausing for a moment, the apprehension he'd seen in her face when she'd stepped from the plane disappeared.

'It's…amazing. Just right out in the middle of nowhere and, boom, there it is.'

'Wait until you see the rig,' he commented. Her slim figure, dressed in beige linen trousers and a pale blue cotton shirt, was outlined to perfection. He decided he'd better not look at her any more. Turning, he started on the last few metres that would bring them to the township, recalling how, when they'd been toe to toe, he'd noticed the presence of only a few wrinkles around her eyes. He'd call them laughter lines rather than wrinkles and realised that the years had been kind to her.

Had she seen many differences in him? Did he look older to her? He certainly felt it but, then, when a man loses his wife in childbirth and ends up a single parent to two adorable but energetic almost three-year-olds, he was bound to feel older...wasn't he? Besides, what did he care what Abigail thought of him? So long as she was a good doctor, so long as she was interested in caring for this community, it didn't matter what she thought of him.

Still, a part of him really wanted to know and that, in itself, disturbed him more than he liked to admit.

CHAPTER TWO

'AH...HERE you are, *ma chérie*,' a woman standing behind the bar at the Yawonnadeere pub called, her French accent unmistakable. 'Joshua, you bring her right over here. I will get her a drink. Ooh-la-la. You poor *chérie*.' The petite Frenchwoman fussed behind the bar, calling something else in French into a room behind her, and a moment later a blond-haired man appeared, dressed in comfortable clothes with an apron tied around his waist.

'You little beauty, Josh. You said you'd get us a female doc to take over from old Doc Turner and you've done it.' He came around the counter of the bar and shook Joshua's hand warmly. Abbey raised an eyebrow at her medical colleague.

'I'm guessing it's more like pure luck that you

actually ended up with a female doctor. PMA will provide who they can, when they can,' Abbey couldn't resist pointing out.

'Ouch,' the man said, looking at her. 'She's got ya there, Josh. Hi. I'm Mark.'

'Abbey.'

He shook her hand then jerked a thumb over his shoulder. 'That's Giselle, my wife. We're both nurses here.'

Abbey was surprised and surveyed her surroundings. 'I was under the impression this was the pub.'

Mark laughed as Joshua walked over to the bar and leaned one arm on the counter, accepting a long cool drink from Giselle. There wasn't anyone else in the pub at this time of the day but Abbey could hear the sounds of children coming from the back somewhere. She presumed Mark and Giselle had a little brood of their own.

'Of course it's the pub, Abbey,' Mark continued. 'The surgery's next door but when things are quiet, Giselle and I work here.'

'And I suppose Joshua's the cook?' Her words were supposed to be facetious.

'Actually, he is a very good cook.' Giselle leaned over and pressed a kiss to Joshua's cheek. 'I like the nights when he cooks because then I can get a real meal, not a pub-style meal. He is such a gourmet.'

Abbey shook her head, unable to believe this strange and completely off-world place she'd arrived at. When she'd signed with PMA, she'd expected a different country with different ways of doing things, but this was still part of Australia and these people were outback Australians. Yet they made her feel as though she came from a completely different planet with the way they ran things. Nurses and doctors working at the pub when it was quiet?

'Are things usually quiet?' Abbey asked as she walked to the bar, keeping a good distance between herself and the ever-present and annoying Joshua, and gratefully accepted the drink Giselle gave her.

'With the pub or the nursing?' Giselle asked. 'The pub is always busy. There will be more people here in about twenty minutes and then we will be busy again.'

'With the nursing, out here, it's either dead as a crocodile's party or all guns blazing,' Mark offered as he joined his wife behind the bar.

Abbey threw Joshua a disbelieving look but there was fear in her eyes. 'Crocodiles have parties?'

He couldn't help but smile and Abbey was glad she was close enough to the bar so she didn't fall down. The action changed his face completely, his blue eyes sparkling instead of shooting daggers at her, his curved mouth showing straight, white teeth instead of surly lips pressed firmly together. Even the laughter lines softened his usual stern expression when he was dealing with her.

'It's just an expression but an odd one at that. Mark just means that no one would go to a crocodile's party, and therefore it—'

'Would be rather dull,' Abbey finished, nodding her head.

'These boys in this town, *chérie,* they do like the joke so don't let yourself be fooled by them, *Okayee*?' Giselle came around the bar as she spoke. 'Come. I show you to your room and you can freshen up. You will be staying in the old doctor's place but the ceiling fans have needed the fixing so you stay here for two nights. *Okayee*? When you come down, I shall make you the most perfect *salade* you've ever had. You like the *salade*? But of course, you are a petite woman,' Giselle continued, answering her own question as they headed up the wooden stairs off to the side of the room. 'Joshua,' she called from the balcony. 'You go get started on the salade Niçoise for Abbey. She is hungry and she needs food.'

'Right you are, Giselle.' Joshua nodded and headed around the bar, disappearing through the door into what Abbey presumed was the kitchen. She followed Giselle in wonder. Joshua could really cook? Had he been able to cook back in medical school? It was then that she realised just how little she really knew of the man. They'd been exhausted students competing to get the best marks for their subjects. They'd been so intent in feeding off each other's successes, egging each other on, badgering each other, that it wasn't until this very moment that she realised she hardly knew him at all. The memory of his smiling face and the way it appeared to have affected her, her knees weakening, her nerves tensing, her gaze drawn to that gorgeous mouth of his…that same gorgeous mouth which had been so close to her own only fifteen minutes ago. The thought that she would have gladly received a kiss from him still rocked her foundations.

No. She was here to do a job, not to explore her confusing emotions where the annoying Joshua Ackles was concerned. The people out here needed her and, more importantly, she needed them. If she was going to find herself, find her place, find what it was she was now meant to do with her life after three years of upheaval, she needed to put her frustrating but gorgeous medical partner out of her mind and focus.

Twenty minutes later, Abbey was feeling far more like a human being. She descended the stairs after having a glorious but quick shower—a necessity given the strict water restrictions the town was under—her still damp hair billowing softly around her shoulders. She was looking forward to having something to eat and then getting to work. She was under no illusions that coming here meant it was time to slacken off and even though it appeared the medical staff in Yawonnadeere Creek preferred to fill their hours playing housekeepers at the pub, it didn't mean she had to.

As Giselle had predicted, where the pub had been empty before, it was now filled. There wasn't a bar stool left free, and the tables were slowly filling up with people as they came in for a midday drink and something to eat.

'Ah, here she is,' Joshua remarked as she walked

towards the counter. He was standing behind the bar, tossing a cocktail shaker with such flourish and flair it was clear he'd done it many times before. 'Make room for the new doctor, Dustin,' he said to a tall man in his early twenties who was sitting on the end bar stool.

Dustin gladly moved, shaking hands with Abbey as he vacated his stool. 'Oh, no. You don't have to,' she quickly protested, shooting Joshua a look that said he didn't have to boot the poor guy off his perch. Joshua merely grinned maddeningly at her but said nothing.

'It's no trouble, Doc,' Dustin replied politely, his American accent surprising her. 'I've got to get to work, at any rate.' He turned and headed over to one of the tables to talk to his friends. Abbey decided not to argue any further and slid onto the stool, leaning her elbows on the bar, her feet dangling like a child's. It made her feel lighter than she'd felt for some time. Maybe coming here *had* been a good decision.

'What can I get you, Abigail?' Joshua said,

still shaking the cocktail shaker. Giselle was also behind the bar, pulling beers and talking to other patrons. There were glorious scents of mouth-watering food coming from the direction of the kitchen.

'Uh…something long and cool.'

'Coming right up.'

'Oh, and as we'll be working together for the next six months, why not call me Abbey?'

Joshua's lips twitched and she knew exactly where his thoughts had gone. 'I remember you telling me that only your friends called you Abbey.' As he spoke, he took a Martini glass from the glass-rack above the bar, coated the rim with red-coloured sugar and poured the contents of the shaker into the glass. 'You then pointed out quite clearly that as you and I would never be friends, if I had to refer to you by name, you much preferred it was Abigail.'

Abbey closed her eyes as he spoke, shaking her head in regret. When she opened her eyes, she found he'd added a cherry and slice of orange to the side of the glass and had even poked a little umbrella through the cherry. She looked at him, feeling slightly ashamed of her younger self. 'I'm sorry, Joshua. What can I say? I was horrible.'

He chuckled. 'Yes, you were.'

'Hey.' She sat up straighter on the bar stool, indignation in her tone. 'I'm trying to be nice here.'

'I know. I was only laughing because I think I was just as bad as you.' He leaned on the bar and added a straw to the glass. 'Try this.'

'Aren't we supposed to be on duty? Having a cocktail for lunch isn't part of my usual routine.'

'Well, you're in the outback now, honey,' he drawled. 'So your routine is going to have to change.' As he spoke Mark came out, carrying a huge bowl which she discovered was filled with her salade Niçoise. 'Besides, it's a mocktail. Non-alcoholic,' he pointed out when she frowned in confusion. 'Now, get eating, *Abbey*, because we need to get out to the rig within the hour.'

'Did you want to share this with me?' she asked, looking down at the enormous dish of salad with all its trimmings. 'Here, pass me another plate and let me scoop some on for you because there's no way I'm going to be able to eat it all.'

Joshua struggled to hide his surprise at her attitude and passed her another plate without question. He hadn't expected Abigail to share and he hadn't expected her to let him call her Abbey. During their time at med school they hadn't really mixed in the same circles, not until their final two years when they'd been forced to be lab partners for a term. Even then, Joshua had been very happy to keep his distance from the prickly Ms Bateman but it just so happened that his best friend and her best friend had started to date, which had meant they had sometimes been thrown together at small social gatherings.

Where she'd always been pleasant and polite with a lot of their set, she'd seen him as an outright rival. Academia had been important to both of them, the competition even more fierce during that final year. Their tutors had suggested that they study together but even that had been out of the question as far as Abbey was concerned. He hadn't been too thrilled at the idea either. How could he possibly beat her marks if they were studying together, sharing techniques and information?

Remembering that, he realised he still needed to keep a professional and personal distance between himself and his new colleague. She was strong willed and competitive, and while he still thought her beautiful and smart, she was here for the community and all he had to do was show her the ropes and work alongside her for six months. Nothing more. She was part of his past, his past long before he'd met Miriam, back before his children had been born and back before...

He pushed the thoughts away. Now was not the time. Needless to say, when his world had been shaken around and turned inside out, he'd realised the best place for him to be was here, in Yawonnadeere Creek. Here, he could raise his children in a loving and supportive environment and his medical duties weren't heavy. Old Dr Turner had shared the load. Would Abbey?

He glanced surreptitiously at her as they sat in silence, eating their lunch. How would she react if he told her what had happened, and what it meant for him now? Would she lord it over him, letting him know that she was far superior, or would she understand?

She'd mentioned earlier that she'd had a terrible few years. Had those years changed her from the gung-ho academic he'd known and loathed? She'd already admitted that she'd been horrible back then and they were now sitting quite amicably, eating lunch together without either one starting a fight.

'You're very quiet,' she said, swallowing a mouthful.

'Pensive,' he returned, finishing his salad and draining his drink.

'Wondering whether we can leave the past in

the past and make this new professional relationship work?'

'Something like that. Finished?'

'Yes.' She put her utensils down and sighed.
'It was delicious so my compliments to whoever
made it, but I definitely can't eat any more.'

'Your compliments are gratefully accepted.'

'Ah, so you did make it. I wasn't sure whether
Giselle was just kidding me when she told you to
get started on the salad.'

'Is that why you insisted on sharing it with me?
To make sure it wasn't poisoned?'

Abbey laughed. 'No, but I wish I'd thought of
that. So you like to cook?'

'I do.'

'Since when?'

He shrugged as he cleared the plates and put
them in the open hatch to the kitchen. 'Since for
ever.'

'Even when we were back in med school?'

'Yep. Cooking calms me down. In our final
year, I did even more baking than before. During

those last weeks of examinations, I baked cookies every night. My mother had to give them away to family and friends we had so many.'

Abbey laughed again. 'That's amazing. I never knew that about you.' She shook her head. 'I guess in some ways we really don't know each other at all.'

Her thoughts mirrored his own and it was another disturbing factor. He didn't want to have things in common with Abigail. He simply wanted another doctor in the area to help him look after the bustling community, which included the personnel from the LPG gas rig. It really wasn't too much to ask, was it? 'Except to know that we can still argue and get on each other's nerves with ease.'

Her smile was bright at his words and for a split second Joshua found himself quite mesmerised by her. Her hair was now dry, floating softly around her face, curling slightly at the ends. Her brown eyes were less tired than before and he realised that a shower and something to eat and drink had definitely gone a long way to making her feel more comfortable. Perhaps it would have been better to have left her cranky and dishevelled—that way at least he wouldn't find her so attractive.

'Amazing, isn't it? After sixteen years of not seeing each other, we can still slip back into the old ways and bicker like not a day has passed.' Abbey tilted her head to the side. 'Does that make us young at heart or old fools?'

Joshua couldn't help but laugh, and shrugged his shoulders. 'Perhaps a bit of both.' He picked up the cloth from the side of the bar and wiped the area down before coming around to stand next to her. 'Ready to leave the relative cool comfort of the pub and head out to the rig?' As he spoke, she noticed Dustin coming around behind the bar to replace Joshua. Did he work here, too? It was a strange situation and she wondered whether anyone and everyone could just slip behind the bar and help out.

'As ready as I'll ever be.' As she spoke, the

door next to the kitchen burst open and in ran two toddlers, the young boy holding a doll, the little girl chasing him. Hard on their heels was a young woman in her early twenties.

'Good. Just give me a second.' Joshua turned and scooped up the little boy without missing a beat. 'What are you doing, monkey?'

'He got my dolly,' the little girl said, and the young woman picked her up.

'Sorry, Josh. They're getting faster every day.'

'That's all right, Rach.' Joshua took the doll from the boy and gave it back to the girl. 'Were you teasing your sister?' he asked, and the little boy shook his head. 'Do you know what teased means?' Joshua asked, and again the boy shook his head. Abbey tried not to laugh. 'It means doing something cheeky when you know Becka will get cross with you.'

The boy nodded his little blond head, then wrapped his arms tightly around Joshua's neck. 'I sorry, Daddy.'

Abbey's eyes widened in shock. 'Daddy?' The

word was out of her mouth before she could stop it. Joshua looked over at her.

'Yes. I am Daddy. This is Jimmy and that's Becka.' He pointed to where Becka was now out of Rach's arms, strutting around the pub as if she owned it, giving kisses to everyone she met. 'They're my twins.'

'Twins.' Abbey was still coming to terms with the fact that Joshua had children. She hadn't pictured him as the fatherly type but as he put the boy back down on the floor, she realised she really hadn't pictured him as married either. She glanced across at the young woman who'd been holding Becka. Was that his wife? If so, she must have been a child bride.

'That's Rach. She's married to Dustin.' He pointed to where the other man was behind the bar. 'They own the pub and help me look after the kids.'

'And you help them cook?'

He shrugged and spread his arms wide, a grin on his face. 'We all help each other out here. It's the outback way.' He headed for the door, collecting his hat and putting it firmly on his head. 'Now that I've touched base with the twins, we can go.'

'Uh…Joshua?'

'Hmm?' He glanced at her over his shoulder. She'd put on her hat and sunglasses, her steps tentative as she started to follow him.

'We don't have to walk to the rig, do we? We are driving, right?'

'Well…we *can* walk if you'd prefer but given the flies and the heat and the time of day, we should have started out about an hour ago.'

'You're teasing,' she murmured, trying not to get cross with him.

'I'm teasing,' he confirmed, calling a cheery goodbye to everyone in the pub and receiving a rowdy response in return before he walked out the door.

'Have fun, Doc,' someone called, and she realised it was aimed at her.

'Oh. I'll try.' She waved, unsure exactly who

she was waving to but wanting to prove that she was happy to be here, even though she thought all of them a glorious bunch of loons.

She continued to follow and watched Joshua, waiting for him to pull out his car keys, waiting for him to divert somewhere else to collect keys from somewhere, but instead he walked across and climbed into a well-used red two-door ute. The windows were down, it was covered in dust and there were two pairs of sunglasses and bits of paper scrunched up in a mess on the dashboard. As she stepped down from the large kerb, the engine purred to life and it was then she realised the keys had been left in the vehicle. She slid into the passenger seat and was pleased when he put the electric windows up and switched on the air-conditioning.

'Do you always leave your keys in your car?' He looked at her for a moment as he slid on a pair of aviator sunglasses.

'Everybody does. Makes it easy to always re-member where your keys are, too.' At her stunned look he laughed. 'Life is different out here, Abbey. No doubt you'll get used to it.'

He switched on the radio and settled back with one hand on the wheel, driving with confidence over the dusty outback roads. There was a stretch of bitumen on the main road for the town but everywhere else was just like open dirt tracks. There were hardly any road signs once he turned off and for a moment she wondered whether he was taking her on a wild-goose chase to show her just how different life out here really was.

It wasn't too long before the skyline started to change from one of gumtrees and shrubs to large steel chimneys, about six or seven of them all shooting up into the sky. The closer they got, the more Abbey could see that the gas rig was far larger than she'd anticipated. She'd looked at photographs on line but they didn't take into account the heat, the flies and the noise that went along with the real-life experience. It was like a small town, in a sort of L shape, a metal monstrous structure on steel girders.

'How many people work here?' she asked.

'Almost three hundred.'

'And you're the only doctor around?'

'*We* are the only doctors around,' he pointed out. 'Yes.'

'And everyone lives in Yawonnadeere?'

'Or the surrounding farms. Not everyone in the district works here, only about eighty percent.'

Abbey was too stunned to say anything else as he pulled up at the gatehouse, showed his identification and parked the car. As they entered the main building, she was still looking around. 'Tell me about our set-up. Do we hold clinics here or do they come to Yawonnadeere?'

'Both. There is an infirmary here and clinics are held a few times a week. Anything else must be by appointment, which Giselle usually arranges.'

'OK.' They stopped at the receptionist's desk where Joshua introduced Abbey, signing her in and requesting an identification tag be made.

'Take these papers to the HOp...' She paused

and looked at Abbey. 'That stands for Head of Operations. Anyway, get Pierre to sign them and return them to me,' Ellen, the receptionist, said. 'Once that's done, I'll get them processed. Look this way, please,' she said to Abbey, and held up a web camera. 'Thanks.'

Abbey put a hand to her head. 'Wait. I wasn't ready.' She smoothed her hair, looking from Ellen to Joshua, all the while straightening her clothes and protesting. 'I can't have that on my ID badge.'

Joshua reached over Ellen's desk and turned the computer monitor around, surveying her photo. 'You look great. Stop worrying.' He straightened and started down the corridor. Abbey followed.

'Stop placating me just because you can't be bothered waiting around. I can't believe you're still so impatient.'

'Me? Impatient? That's a laugh.' He stopped outside a door and knocked twice. 'I seem to recall that you were far more impatient than I ever was.' He lowered his voice slightly. 'Remember when we organised a surprise party for Sammy and you jumped up and yelled "Surprise" earlier than everyone else?'

Abbey couldn't believe the embarrassment that swamped her at the memory. 'How do you re-member things like that?'

'Because it was funny.'

'You're embarrassing me. It was a mistake. I thought I heard her walk in and that's—'

The door they were standing in front of was wrenched open and Abbey jumped, startled at the suddenness of the action. 'Come on in,' the owner of the office said. 'Pierre Knowles.' He reached out a hand to Abbey and when she shook it, she noted it was cold and clammy. He was a tall man, whose hair was more grey than the sandy blond she could see in places and he was a little overweight. 'You must be the new doc. Hi, Josh. Come on in, both of you. Please sit down.'

Pierre's words were brisk and to the point, as though he really didn't have a lot of time. The man had three different phones on his desk and another one strapped to his waist. There was a fresh cup of coffee on his desk and a cupcake on a plate, yet neither had been touched. There was a bottle of water which Pierre now reached for, taking a sip. Abbey's doctor'senses started tingling as she observed him.

'What were you two arguing about, standing outside my door?' Pierre asked, and as he walked back behind his desk, Abbey clinically studied his gait, finding that he was a little hunched over. When he sat down, she was positive she saw him wince.

'Nothing.'

'The past.'

They spoke at the same time and at Pierre's raised eyebrows Joshua quickly filled him in. 'We went to the same medical school.'

'You dated?'

'No.' Again, they spoke together, Abbey's word more vehement than Joshua's. She didn't want anyone to get the wrong idea of what their past relationship had been…even though back then he'd looked just as gorgeous as he did now. That wasn't the point.

'We were more like…rivals,' Joshua finished.

Abbey continued to study Pierre's face, now noticing that his brow was peppered with sweat. The heat in the office wasn't too bad and neither was Pierre overdressed, his crew uniform fitting him snugly.

'Are you feeling all right?' As she asked the question, her mind flicked through different scenarios.

'I'm fine.' He took a sip of water. 'Now, I know you've just flown in this morning but I asked Josh to bring you down straight away so that you can get a good look at the rig, familiarise yourself with the infirmary and generally touch base, as well as get the red tape taken care of.' He held out his hand for the forms Joshua was holding and as he accepted them Abbey again noticed how weak Pierre was. She glanced across at Joshua, to see if he'd noticed anything.

When he glanced back at her, she knew he had. There was something wrong.

Pierre took another small sip from the water bottle. She looked at his lips and saw that they were cracked and a little white, even though there was sweat on his upper lip. Dehydrated. The circles around his eyes were dark but where she would have initially thought the man wasn't getting enough sleep, no doubt due to the stress of his job, she now wondered whether he wasn't sleeping due to being in constant pain.

He hadn't touched the cupcake and his coffee was starting to cool. Pierre was still talking, explaining to her the intricacies of the rig, but she was only half listening. She'd have to ask Joshua about it later.

'Old Doc Turner was a good doctor. She won't be at all easy to replace.'

'I'm not looking to replace anyone. I'm only here to assist Joshua as best I can for the next six months. Excuse me, are you sure you're feeling all right?' Abbey asked again. 'You don't look so good.' She was out of her chair and heading around to the other side of the desk, intent on taking a closer look at the man.

'I told you, I'm fine. There's no need to start fussin—' Pierre broke off from what he was saying.

'You're not fine. I knew it.' Joshua was up and around the other side of the desk, both doctors surveying Pierre closely. 'He hasn't been eating all that well the past few weeks.'

'What? Of course I have,' Pierre blustered.

'I've been watching you and Ellen has been giving me reports,' Joshua said. 'Look at that cup-cake. Usually you can't resist cakes and devour them within minutes of seeing them. Not so today.'

'He's dehydrated.' Abbey placed a hand to Pierre's forehead. 'He's burning up. We need to get him to the surgery or infirmary or whatever it is you do in this place when people are ill.'

'I don't need to go to the—' Pierre tried again

but broke off, doubling over and clutching his abdomen.

Joshua grabbed one of the phones on the desk and quickly called for help. 'Ellen, organise for a stretcher to be brought the HOp's office. Call the pub, tell Mark and Giselle to prep for surgery and get the helicopter ready. We need to transfer Pierre to the surgery, stat.'

With that, he returned his attention to Abbey.

'Let's get him on the floor,' Abbey instructed. 'Loosen his clothing. You said he's been off his food?'

'I noticed it at the beginning of last week. Since then I've been keeping an eye on him.'

She began carefully palpating the man's abdomen and when she pressed on the lower right side, Pierre nearly passed out from the pain.

'Appendicitis,' the two doctors said in unison.

'He needs to be in surgery, ASAP,' she said. 'Can you organise that? Where would he go? Adelaide?'

'No time to transfer him anywhere. He's too far gone.'

'What are you suggesting?'

'We need to operate.'

'Where? All I've seen of Yawonnadeere is the pub.'

'There's a small operating theatre out the back of the surgery in town. We'll transfer him there by chopper. Mark will anaesthetise, Giselle will be theatre nurse and you and I, Dr Bateman, will be…well, I guess we'll be the surgeons.'

As he said the words, trying to inject some humour into the situation, Abbey noticed a tightening of his smile, a loss of colour in his face and hesitation behind his eyes. She'd seen that look on Joshua before. When they'd first been assigned together as lab partners, he'd taken unnecessary risks with their experiment and although she'd argued with him, demanding they follow the set procedure, he hadn't listened. As a result, they'd almost failed that part of the module and she'd been furious. Yet just before they'd been marked, she'd noticed the same pallor and hesitation that he was displaying now.

'Are you qualified for surgery?'

'General surgery, yes, although out here you become a "bitsa" doctor. Bits of this and bits of that.' They continued to monitor Pierre as they spoke.

'Are you OK to operate, Joshua? He is your friend, after all.'

Joshua's smile instantly disappeared. 'There's no one else, Abbey. Out here, we're it, and whether the patient is your friend or your family, you have to do something. That's just the way it is.'

There was a vehemence to his words that she hadn't expected but his attitude also told Abbey there was far more going on in his life than he was admitting.

Shaking her head, she had to wonder, what on earth she'd got herself into.

CHAPTER THREE

PIERRE was transferred from the helicopter, which had landed as close to the town centre as possible, to the back of a ute Mark had ready. They drove to the surgery, which was situated next door to the pub, and it was then Abbey realised there was also a house attached to the rear. Was that where she would end up living or was that where Joshua lived with his children… and his wife?

Children. She still couldn't believe he had children. The question remained, though—where was his wife? Was he divorced? Was she simply interstate? Perhaps she worked out at the mine? What unsettled Abbey more was the way Joshua had looked at her earlier. They'd been close, their emotions had been heightened and he'd looked as though he'd wanted to kiss her.

He may have flaws, he may annoy her from here to kingdom come, but she'd never pegged him for a philanderer. One of their friends had been two-timing a girl back in med school and both she and Joshua had agreed it was wrong. In fact, it was about the only time she ever remembered them agreeing on anything.

'Bring Pierre in,' Giselle called from the rear of the surgery. 'I am all set up and ready for him.'

Abbey helped Mark and Giselle transfer Pierre to the operating table while Joshua went to the sink and started scrubbing. She kept a close eye on her colleague as Giselle and Mark took care of the patient, getting him anaesthetised. Joshua still didn't look one hundred per cent and as she joined him at the small scrub sink, she couldn't help but let her concern out.

'You can do this, right?'

'Of course I can,' he snapped. 'What makes you doubt me?'

'You're as pale and as skittish as you were for our first experiment as lab partners.'

Joshua stared at her for a moment before his face hardened, his eyes turning positively glacial. 'I need to focus.' With that, he returned to vigorously scrubbing his hands.

'I'm guessing we don't have a laparoscope?' Abbey asked the room in general.

'*Non, chérie,*' Giselle replied. 'Joshua will remove the appendix via laparotomy. Yes?' she asked.

'Of course.' Joshua snapped again, and it was then Abbey realised he wasn't just mad with her. Something wasn't right. She had no idea what it was but at the moment all that mattered was Pierre. Everything else could wait. The last thing they needed now was more tension in the room, especially between the medical staff, who needed to be united in order to save Pierre's life.

She decided it was up to her to keep the peace, preferring that if Joshua was going to get cross at anyone, it would be her. 'I know you're concentrating, Joshua, but I thought I should let you know that I've never assisted with a laparotomy before.'

His response was to grunt.

'If you wouldn't mind talking me through whatever it is you need me to do, I'd appreciate it. If I understand what's going on, I'm not going to make any errors.'

There was a pause, then one clipped word. 'Fine.'

Was it her imagination, or had he mellowed in that one instant? Had he thought she'd be picking on him, pointing out any mistakes he might be making? This wasn't an experiment in a lab, this was a man's life, and she would do anything to have the next hour or so run as smoothly as possible. Being an A and E specialist, she was used to dealing with multiple traumas as well as staff who were on edge. If everyone was calm and worked together as a team, there were usually few complications. Yet if people were antagonistic towards each other… No. It was up to her at the moment to keep the peace, to take her place as assistant to the surgeon and do what Joshua needed her to do.

What she didn't need was to be quite so aware of him as they stood side by side at the scrub sink. His warmth, his scent, his nearness all radiated towards her. He was most definitely having an unwanted effect on her. That was the last thing she needed as it definitely wasn't making her feel calm and collected.

She was off men. She didn't want to be around them, not in a romantic light, even if they were old acquaintances. She'd made the decision to leave her old life behind her in Sydney and work for PMA. After the chemotherapy, after her hair had grown back, after she'd stopped feeling so sick, after fielding sympathetic pity glances from colleagues for so long, the need for a change, to find where her new life might be, had led Abbey here. Now, three years after her initial surgery, she found herself as far away from her past problems as she could be, only to be faced with a new problem. Her increasing awareness of the man beside her—a man who could well be married.

Frowning, she looked back at her hands and scrubbed them even more vigorously than was called for.

Joshua finished scrubbing and kneed open a cupboard before reaching in to retrieve a sterile towel to wipe his hands. He'd noticed Abbey's frown and wondered if it was there because of him or because of the situation she now found herself in. Perhaps she was just nervous about the operation they were going to perform? As they'd stood there, side by side at the sink, Joshua's focus had changed from mentally going through the surgery he'd performed many times in the past to the woman standing next to him.

To say he was aware of her was an understatement. Her scent was one of sweet sunshine and hope. Was that possible? Could Abbey Bateman bring him hope? He never would have thought it before now but he had to keep reminding himself that they were different people now from who they'd been back then. Still, he felt an awareness between them and that in itself was disturbing. He wasn't in the market for another relationship. He'd completely failed at his marriage, in so many ways, that he most certainly wouldn't recommend it to anyone. However, the way Abbey made him feel only seemed to be growing the more time he spent with her. Were these feelings simply residuals? Something left over? Or were they a burning pilot light?

They both continued getting ready, doing what needed to be done, Giselle attending to Pierre while Mark administered the anaesthetic. Abbey glanced at Joshua again, hating the fact that she was so aware of him. How on earth was she supposed to concentrate when he was standing right next to her? She knew it was no one's fault that she was experiencing these emotions but if there was one thing she liked to be, it was in control.

Her life had been turned upside down and shaken all around. She'd had no control over being attacked by ovarian cancer. She'd had no control over the radical surgery she'd required. She'd had no control over the chemotherapy treatments she'd had to endure, which had included losing her hair. She'd had no control over what the disease had done to her body but she'd worked excessively hard to ensure she coped with the emotional upheaval. Even now, some days she simply wanted to curl into the foetal position and cry.

Control? She'd had absolutely no control over what had happened to her in the past and she'd vowed, once the chemo had finished and she'd been given a clean bill of health, that she would structure her life so neatly that wherever possible she would have some comforting level of control.

This was most definitely *not* one of those situations, and as they continued to gown and glove up, Abbey sent up a silent prayer that everything would go according to plan before she took her place beside Joshua. They all needed to be focused and as she saw that Joshua's face was still quite pale, she realised it was up to her to ensure they all stayed on track.

Giselle had removed Pierre's clothing and as the Frenchwoman scrubbed, Abbey swabbed and draped the patient. Joshua was busy looking over the instruments, mentally organising them, but he kept glancing at his anaesthetised friend. There was a strange look in his eyes, one that seemed to reflect fear and pain. Why was he so nervous about operating? What on earth had happened to him to make him like this? It was as though he was simply a shadow of his former self.

'Patient's anaesthetised,' Mark announced. 'Ready when you are, Doctors.' He paused, then looked at his friend. 'You all right to do this, Josh?'

'He is fine,' Giselle answered for him. 'Can you not see he is fine? He is concentrating. He is ready.'

Mark shrugged. Abbey watched Joshua, certain now there was something wrong. He glared at his friends, looking as though he was ready to explode. She needed to step in, to do something, to keep them all calm.

'You know, I never thought to ask,' she interjected, her tone light. 'Do you operate left- or right-handed? I, for example, am left-handed but when I'm working, I tend to do everything right-handed. Did you ever notice that back when we were lab partners, Joshua? I didn't pick up on it until my first year in A and E.'

'I noticed it,' he remarked. 'I was always impressed with your ambidexterity but as commenting on it would have been considered a compliment, I refrained from saying anything.'

'Really?' Her eyes sparkled with delight at his words. 'Wow. You were impressed with me back then.'

'Great.' Joshua exhaled slowly and Abbey saw him visibly start to relax a little. 'Now you're going to get an inflated ego.'

'I'll try to keep it under control but only while we're in here. The instant this procedure is done,

I'm going to bug you to tell me other ways I impressed you in the past.'

She was impressing him now because he could well see how she was diffusing his tension. 'Then I'd better take my time with the surgery, hoping you might forget.'

'There's always that,' she said as she glanced at him. He was looking down at Pierre, supine and anaesthetised on the table, waiting. 'Let's get this operation under way.' Abbey's words were soft and encouraging. 'We can do this,' she assured him.

He was sweating and she knew it wasn't from the heat in the room. The operating room's large bright light was shining above the patient, casting light where it was needed, but she also doubted that it could have made Joshua sweat as much as he was now. He was covered in a fine sheen and it was starting to soak into the rim of his theatre cap.

'Joshua?' Abbey took in his pale pallor, keeping her tone calm.

No answer.

She watched him swallow, his Adam's apple sliding up and down his throat, before he opened his mouth and licked his lips. She tried again. 'Dry throat? Need some water?'

There was something most definitely wrong and Abbey wished to goodness she knew what it was. They needed to focus. 'Joshua? I need you to focus because right now Pierre has more colour than you.' Abbey kept her voice firm, needing to get through to him. 'Come on. You won't let your friend die and I need you to help me. Just like when we were lab partners. We can do this. Together. Remember?'

'I remember.' The two words were spoken softly but rather hoarsely. Joshua cleared his throat again and dragged in a deep breath before looking intently into Abbey's eyes. At that moment it was as though they had a firm con-nection. Working together, because they had to. Focusing and getting the job done, because they had to.

When next he spoke, there was firmness to his words. 'Let's do this.'

Abbey had no idea what type of war had just gone on inside Joshua's head but, thankfully, she'd been able to bring him back from wherever he'd gone. Returning her thoughts to her patient, she tried to focus and relax as he held out his hand for the scalpel.

Joshua made a neat incision and she listened to his calm voice letting her know what he was doing so she could assist effectively.

'Kidney dish,' he said, and soon the offending little organ was out of Pierre's body and in the kidney dish. Giselle examined it closely.

'Now, I'm going to check around the area to ensure there aren't any other signs of trouble,' Joshua said, his calm voice floating over the room as he gave her more specific instructions.

'It is intact,' Giselle announced, and Abbey nodded. 'It is septic, though. It is no wonder this man was in so much pain. Peritonitis wasn't far away.'

'Looks as though every thing's fine.' Joshua breathed with relief and when their gazes met across the operating table, their eyes twinkled with appreciation and she knew they were both smiling beneath their masks. It was then that Abbey realised she could stand there and look in to his eyes for ever. He had the ability to mesmerise her with just one look, and a spark of the tingles she'd ignored all those years ago started deep her in belly before spreading throughout her entire body. Abbey sighed and then straightened as she realised where her thoughts had just taken her.

'Uh…Mark. How's he holding up?' Joshua asked, looking away from Abbey. How could she make even scrubs look sexy? It was wrong. When he'd stared into her eyes, he'd been surprised to see a spark of delight there. Did she feel it, too?

'Brilliant.'

'Good. Well, all right, then. I guess I'm ready to suture this wound closed,' he stated, satisfied that the immediate threat to Pierre's life had now been eliminated. Their patient was fine. Everyone had performed admirably, pulling through as they always did in an emergency, and had saved the day. He hated to admit it but he couldn't have done it without Abbey's know-how and steady guidance.

Finally, they were done and Giselle put a clean bandage on the wound. Mark was ready to start reversing the anaesthetic and the entire atmosphere in the room was one of great relief. Abbey started tidying the instruments, doing a final count before getting them into the steriliser. As she worked alongside Joshua, she tried hard to ignore him as best as she could, trying not to be so aware of his manly scent or the way the heat from his body seemed to ignite her blood, making it pump faster with newly awakened desire.

Finally, she could take it no longer. 'I'm just going to get some air,' she said after degowning, and walked out to the front verandah of the building. There were a few chairs scattered here and there, along with two little plastic chairs. It was then Abbey realised that although this was the doctor's surgery, it was also Joshua's residence. These were the chairs where he probably sat at night, along with his cute little twins, watching as the sun disappeared and the stars came out.

She leaned against the rail of the old weatherboard home, trying to get control over her wayward thoughts. She wasn't supposed to be attracted to him. He was her annoying nemesis from medical school. Yet half a day in his company had proved that that wasn't the case at all.

She heard the front screen door open and close but she didn't need to look over her shoulder to know who it was. She could sense him, hear his soft footfalls coming closer. Shifting backwards, she inadvertently tripped on a small plastic chair and would have fallen had it not been for Joshua's firm, strong arms coming about her, catching her before disaster could strike.

'Are you all right?' The words were spoken softly, his mouth still quite close to her ear as he shifted the small chair out of the way with his foot. He liked the way she felt in his arms but he also knew it was wrong. He was disastrous at relationships and while Abbey had never been one of his favourite people in the past, it would do no good to get involved with her in a personal way now. Still, one or two more moments wouldn't hurt, right? He breathed in deeply, his cheek resting near her hair, the silky strands soft against his skin as her scent wound itself about him.

Abbey was struggling to right herself, her legs twisted, her upper body pressed up against Joshua as he held her firmly. It was a nice sensation. To be held, to be supported by someone. She'd taken so much on her shoulders during the past few years that it wasn't until that moment, when she leaned against him, that she realised how tired she was. Tired of being brave. Tired of being in control. Tired of being alone.

She swallowed over the sudden lump in her throat and was astonished to find tears were once more threatening to make themselves known. What was it about Joshua and compassion? This was the second time he'd offered it and this was the second time she'd been close to tears.

'My kids are as messy as their old man,' he murmured, his mouth near her ear, his breath causing goose bumps to scatter down her spine. Abbey momentarily closed her eyes. She didn't want his yummy voice, or his firm, sexy body, or his hypnotic eyes to distract her, especially when she was attempting to get herself under control.

She glanced up and shifted away, wondering if she'd imagined his reluctance in letting her go. She sat in one of the chairs, not trusting her legs to hold her up, especially given the embrace they'd just shared.

'So…uh…where will I be living once they fix the ceiling fans?'

Joshua leaned one hip on the rail and pointed across the road at an old weatherboard home that was almost identical to his, except smaller. 'That's where Dr Turner used to live. She and her husband came out here long before the rig arrived bringing with it mass expansion of the area. This used to just be the surgery but when I decided to stay, the town decided to build me a residence out the back.'

'Next door to the pub?'

He grinned. 'Ideal location. Close to the beer and cold drinks.'

'And the kitchen.' Abbey's smile increased. 'I still can't believe you like to cook.'

'Believe it, honey. Besides, it's also close for Rach to take care of the kids.'

'And when the pub's busy? Who looks after your kids then?'

Joshua shrugged. 'The whole town, actually. It's a strange situation but my kids belong to the whole town.' He glanced down at his feet, his tone becoming less free. 'They were born here. In this very house.'

'Really?'

'They were only five weeks premature but for twins, that's still not good. Dr Turner was an expert at dealing with preemies, though. She'd done her fair share of deliveries and dealt with quite a lot of neonates in her time.'

'How old are they?'

'They'll be three on Sunday.'

'This Sunday?'

Joshua nodded. 'I am in full party-planning mode.'

'You don't sound too thrilled. I thought children's birthday parties were supposed to be grand, glorious affairs with lots of lollies and cakes.'

'That sounds about right. They've both been putting in their orders for cakes and presents.'

She smiled at that, but Joshua seemed tired even thinking about it. 'They're gorgeous children, Joshua. Both so fair with big blue eyes. They must be a handful, though.'

'They are.' His nod was emphatic.

Abbey swallowed, knowing she needed to ask the question but not sure she wanted to know the answer. 'And their mother?'

Joshua looked at her for a long moment before

nodding slowly. 'Best you hear the gossip from me. Everyone in the town knows what happened.'

'You don't have to tell me if you—'

'It's fine.' His words were back to being brisk and he stood and walked to the opposite side of the verandah.

'Look, Joshua, you don't have to talk to me if you don't want to but I won't deny that I am very curious. You've also just gone quite pale again. Not as white as you were in there but still a close second.'

Joshua walked over and sat in the chair opposite her. He was silent, not volunteering any information but Abbey could see it brewing and bubbling away beneath the surface.

He'd listened intently to her words, knowing she was right. This was Abbey, not some strange doctor who had come to town. While their past had been more antagonistic than supportive, he also knew he could trust her. There had always been a buzz flowing between them, even back in medical school, but both had been too dedicated to their future careers to do anything about it. The fact that the zing was still flowing between them over sixteen years later was astounding. He owed her the truth.

'You want to know what happened?' he asked, his tone as cold as stone. Abbey shivered a little. 'You want to know why I live here, hiding in the outback so I don't have to deal with the stress of surgery all day, every day?' He shrugged. 'The answer, Dr Bateman, is quite simple.' Joshua paused and breathed out slowly. 'I killed my wife.'

CHAPTER FOUR

THE words were spoken very matter-of-factly and Abbey could do nothing except sit there and gape at him.

'I'm sorry?' There was a confused and puzzled frown on her face. 'Did you just say you *killed* your wife?'

'I apologise for the blunt delivery.' He shrugged again. 'It's the truth. I had to…operate on my wife and she died.'

'Why on earth were you operating on your wife?' The question was out of Abbey's mouth before she could stop it. 'I mean, it's against hospital policy to have a surgeon operate on family members.'

'You know that. I know that. But sometimes circumstances are what they are.'

He was talking in riddles and Abbey's frown only increased. It was then she recalled him saying that out here, whether the patient was friend or family, it was up to the doctor to do something.

'How long have you been a doctor here? You said your children were born here?'

He could see Abbey was putting two and two together. 'That's right. In this very house, almost three years ago.'

'Which means that something happened to your wife and you were forced to operate and…' She stopped, her mind whirring. 'Oh, no. Joshua.' Her face radiated pain and disbelief and he could see she'd guessed his secret. 'Your wife died in childbirth?' As he slowly nodded, her heart went out to him. He'd said the twins would be turning three next week, which would also bring the anniversary of his wife's death.

She thought over Mark and Giselle's concern for him in the operating theatre. 'How often have you operated since your wife passed away?'

'Today was the first time I took the lead.

Generally, Dr Turner would operate and I'd assist.'

'No wonder you were nervous and concerned.'

'You said I was pale.'

'You were. I thought at one point we'd have to peel you up off the floor.'

'I'm glad you didn't have to.'

She smiled at him as she swatted a fly. A nice breeze had come up and as her hair was still tied up from Theatre, she angled her neck to the side, allowing the air to circulate around her. It felt soothing, refreshing, and it was as though the wind was blowing away the past, blowing away the words Joshua had spoken, the pain and anguish that had been in his tone. While she could admit he could still rile her quite easily, what he'd just told her about his wife made her feel closer to him. Pain, she understood. Personal pain, she understood. Professional pain, she understood.

They may not have trodden the same path but their experiences had now led them to the same place. They were both recovering from their worlds being blown apart and as she tilted her head the other way, still watching Joshua closely, she was struck with an overwhelming urge to touch him, to reassure him that she really did know the emotions he was feeling. The circumstances may have been different but the feelings of loss, of power, of dejection were the same.

She leaned forward in her chair and placed her hand on his. 'What you accomplished today, stepping forward and operating on Pierre, was fantastic, Joshua. You didn't shy away from the situation. Instead, you pulled yourself together and did what needed to be done. That's amazing.'

Joshua looked down at her hand on his, her soft, smooth skin bringing heat and heightened awareness to his roughened, dry one. She wasn't offering him sympathy, as he'd expected. Usually when people learned of Miriam's death, they were sad and upset and concerned, and while he'd witnessed those sorts of emotions in Abbey's eyes as she had drawn her own conclusions about his past, she was now offering encouragement and praise.

As he looked into her big brown eyes, he caught a glimpse of her own pain. She, too, had been troubled by something life changing in the past. It wasn't the first clue he'd received to bring him to that conclusion but her heartfelt words, her touch, the way she was letting him know that she was there for him…it was all becoming too much.

'It's not a big deal,' he murmured, standing and walking to the rail, turning his back to her, needing the distance, the space, the divide. He'd been fine sitting near her, doing a great job of keeping himself under control, until she'd touched him. He'd stared at her neck when she'd angled it to the side, the breeze lightly teasing a few loose tendrils, and it had only been through superhuman strength that he hadn't followed through on his urge to swoop down and press a trail of butterfly kisses all over her enticingly, glorious skin.

'But it is,' she insisted. 'You've had a breakthrough. That's huge.'

He still kept his back to her. 'But will I be able to do it again? If there's another emergency, if there's another situation that requires me to step forward and operate, will I be able to do it again?' The confusion in his voice only made Abbey's belief in him increase. She moved to him, standing beside him, putting her hand on his shoulder and pushing slightly so that he was forced to look at her.

'You know me, Joshua. I don't give out compliments, I don't build people's egos up, I'm not a people pleaser. We've been lab partners in the past, we've been rivals, we've fed off the overly heightened sense of competition that exists in scholastic environments, but through all of that, as well as what I've seen of you today, I know for a fact that you are a good and very clever man. You care for this community and you'll keep on caring for them for a long time to come. You're a general surgeon who has found a way to cope with challenges life has thrown at you. Being here, in Yawonnadeere Creek, doesn't make you a failure. Caring for people in a remote location doesn't make you any less of a brilliant doctor than the surgeons who work excessively long hours in a sterile, impersonal hospital environment in the city.' She swallowed, wanting him to know that she admired him, that she was proud of him and that she was now ready to embrace her six months here, hoping the town could show her what her new purpose in life was, just as it had shown Joshua his.

'You may think you're here, in this town, in this place, because you're hiding from the world. That's not so. You're here because these people need you. Today, Pierre needed you and you didn't let him down. Sure, Dr Turner may have helped you out by taking the lead, by performing any surgery, especially if she knew you had an aversion to it. But perhaps during those years, that was what you needed her to do so you could heal. Today it was time to move on and you did.' She gave his shoulder a little squeeze. 'Again, I reiterate that what you did today, the ghosts you faced…it was amazing.'

To have her standing there, touching him, praising him. To have her so close that if he reached out and hauled her into his arms, as he was so desperately wanting to do, he felt she wouldn't pull away. Her words had meant a lot to him and where he'd heard similar words from his friends here in Yawonnadeere, hearing them from Abbey, from someone who hadn't particularly liked him in the past, was nothing short of enlightening.

She'd said he was amazing and right now, at this point in time, he was actually starting to feel amazing. He wouldn't let it go to his head, he doubted Abbey would allow that. Where she was now praising him for his accomplishments, he knew she would have no hesitation whatsoever in bringing him down a peg or two if she felt he deserved it.

And that was where she was so incredibly different from his wife. While he was the first to admit that his marriage hadn't been the strongest in the world, that his relationship with Miriam even before she'd become pregnant had most certainly needed a lot of work, he'd been willing and determined to work on it, to provide his children with a two-parent home, where Mum and Dad made every effort to get along.

But when he'd told Abbey that he'd killed his wife, he hadn't only been talking about the C-section he'd had to perform. He'd been thinking about the way he'd talked Miriam into having children in the first place. It had been one of the areas in their two-year marriage that had caused the most contention. Miriam had been more than happy with it being just the two of them. They had been free, able to do whatever they'd wanted. They had both been doctors, both earning good money and, therefore, the world had been their oyster. Joshua had needed more. He'd talked her into having children and with great reluctance she'd agreed to have one.

'And only one,' he could recall her saying, holding up one lone finger to emphasise her point. When she'd discovered she was expecting twins, she'd been furious. 'I'm not quitting my job, Josh. You can take care of them or they can go to day care. I have my career to focus on and I've already taken this year off in order to be an incubator.'

That had been his wife…the wife he hadn't been able to save. All of these images flashed like lightning in his mind as he stood there, looking at Abbey who was validating his life. He simply wasn't used to it, used to having someone stand before him and tell him, in earnest, that they believed in him. Abbey Bateman was quite a woman.

She was a beautiful woman too, but he was starting to realise it wasn't just what was on the outside that mattered. It had been a pure physical attraction that had seen him end up married to Miriam and he'd vowed since her death to try and look at people—not just women but everyone—for who they were, rather than how they looked.

He'd already noted that Abbey didn't wear any wedding rings but tonight he'd double-check her PMA file, which listed her marital status. For some reason, it was becoming important that he learn more about her. As he looked down into her face, her hand still on his shoulder, he realised she didn't wear any jewellery at all, except for a small silver chain around her neck with a diamond-studded pendant in the shape of an O.

'Joshua?'

He'd been quiet for so long that she was now starting to look concerned. 'Thanks, Abbey.'

She smiled, rubbing her thumb up and down on his shoulder, the heat from her palm causing his awareness of her to continue to increase. Did she have any idea how she was affecting him? He could no longer deny that in the past he'd found Abbey attractive but, given that they'd argued a lot of the time, he'd been able to control those wayward feelings. Now she was here, in front of him, touching him, being kind to him.

Her sweet scent was becoming familiar to

him and he liked it. The need to reach out and touch her, to feel the silky strands of her hair, the warmth of her neck, the taste of her lips. He wanted to do all of that and more, but he also knew it was wrong. Colleagues. They had to remember they were going to be colleagues for the next six months. She'd burst back into his life with a vengeance and he was no doubt having trouble controlling his urges because of their past. He had to remain focused. He had his life here in Yawonnadeere, with his friends and his children. He was respected and well liked. That had been enough for him during these past few years and it would continue to be enough for him in the future. Besides, although he and Abbey were quite harmonious at the moment, within a matter of minutes they would probably be arguing again.

'We'd best go check on Pierre,' he murmured a moment later, edging back from her touch. Abbey dropped her arm back to her side, a little puzzled by his quick shift in attitude. He'd been so vulnerable, so pained, so filled with regret as he'd told her about his wife, about his children, about his past. She knew it couldn't have been easy for him to open up to her, especially as their past relationship had been one of antagonism. He had made her feel as though a different sort of bond was starting to develop between them.

Now he seemed to be backing away from her at a rate of knots. Perhaps she'd made him feel too vulnerable? As she watched him head back into the surgery, the screen door bouncing shut after him, she was sure that was the reason. That had to be it because otherwise it could mean that something else had just been going on between them. And Abbey wasn't sure she was ready to deal with that.

The fact that she was all too aware of him, that from the moment she'd realised the man she would be working with, here in Yawonnadeere Creek, was Joshua Ackles, the old buried feelings she'd had towards him had begun to surface. She remembered all too clearly telling one of their friends, who'd had a crush on Joshua, that while he was most certainly good looking, a girl also had to take into consideration what was inside the package.

Today she'd seen many sides to the man. Friend, father and foe. She smiled at the last one and shook her head. How could she even think of having any sort of feelings other than professional ones for her new colleague? It was impossible. Her life was in a state of flux and she'd come here to try and sort that out. Getting romantically involved with anyone, let alone Joshua, wasn't going to do her any good.

Never being able to have children, to have a life grow within her, was something she'd lived with every day for the past three years and whenever she allowed herself to think about it, she usually ended up fixating on it so much she would come crashing down into an untidy mess. It wouldn't help anyone in this town if their new medic was a basket case and right now she had a patient who still needed care.

She headed back inside and heard the rest of the team discussing Pierre's transfer details. Pierre was conscious but still extremely groggy from the anaesthetic. It didn't, she realised, stop him from interjecting as the others spoke.

'I don't want to go to Adelaide,' Pierre insisted. 'I'm the HOp and my place is on the rig.'

'No one is indispensable,' Joshua pointed out calmly to his friend.

'We can take him,' Mark said, glancing across at his wife. 'We can stay overnight in Adelaide and catch a flight back with Morgan in the morning.'

'Ooh, Markie,' Giselle purred, walking over to her husband and running her hand over his broad shoulders and then down his back to pinch his butt. 'What a superb idea that is.'

'Hey, cut that out,' Joshua warned with good-natured teasing. 'First and foremost, this is a medical transfer.'

Mark winked at his wife and kissed her cheek. 'We promise to be professional.'

'Until Pierre is settled in *l'hôpital*,' Giselle agreed.

'OK. Sounds like a plan. I'll get the rig's chopper organised to transfer the three of you.'

'How long will he need to be in Adelaide?' Abbey asked, wanting to familiarise herself with the protocols.

'Overnight.' The answer came from Pierre and Joshua gave a short burst of laughter as his answer.

'You'll be in for the next three days,' he told his friend.

'What?' Pierre blustered, moving around as though he was trying to sit up. Abbey was at his side in an instant, as was Joshua, both of them putting a hand to Pierre's shoulder to keep him still.

'Settle,' Joshua said.

'Why? Why can't I stay here?' Pierre demanded, although there was less fight to his tone and more drowsiness instead.

'Because you need to rest,' Abbey supplied. 'I doubt you'll do that if you stay in town.'

'Besides, the only place you can stay is here,' Joshua added. 'And you'll get no rest with my kids in the house. They're still not sleeping through the night and don't even get me started on what happens if one of them wets the bed. Who knew toilet training would be so hard?'

Pierre settled at this news but it was clear he didn't like it. 'Then why do I have to go with the lovebirds? At least send me with the pretty new doctor.'

'Uh-uh,' Joshua continued. 'The pretty new doctor has to stay in town and learn her new job. If I take you, I'll have to bring the twins along and that wouldn't make for a fun trip either. So you see, the arrangements are made and there's nothing you can do about it. Just lie there and relax, mate.'

Pierre closed his eyes but the curl of his lip told Abbey he still wasn't happy with the arrangements. 'I hope both your kids wet the bed tonight,' she thought she heard him slur as he drifted off again.

'Here's hoping they don't,' Joshua retorted. 'I'm sick of stripping beds and washing sheets all the time.'

Abbey chuckled. 'At least the weather out here is conducive to getting them dry.'

'That's about the only good thing,' he returned, momentarily allowing the lovely sound of her laughter to wash over him. Why was it that just when he'd finally got himself under control once more, she found another way to affect him? 'Come on, Abbey. I'll take you through the procedure for transferring a patient.' Joshua headed from the room, not waiting for her, needing a few seconds to pull himself together once more.

Thankfully, by the time she walked into his consulting room and sat down opposite him, the desk firmly between them, Joshua was back in control. They worked through the transfer step by step. About an hour later, the helicopter pilot walked into the surgery.

'Ute's outside, ready to transfer the HOp to the helicopter, Josh.'

'Beauty. Let's go get Pierre.' They headed back to the operating room where Mark was still monitoring Pierre, Giselle having gone to pack them an overnight bag.

'You're a bully, Joshua Ackles,' Pierre mumbled when he saw the pilot, and received a rich laugh from his friend. Abbey tried to ignore the deep throaty sound as Joshua's laughter washed over her. When she looked at the man, the grin spread across his lips changed his features so much. His blue eyes were bright and welcoming. Abbey tried not to gasp at the sight and worked hard to ignore the tingles that spread through her body.

Abbey returned her attention back to Pierre's transfer and made sure he wasn't in any pain so he could endure the helicopter ride without discomfort. 'You'll do fine and we'll have you back here in next to no time,' she told him.

'Thank you, Abbey,' Pierre said, and while his tone was still rather gruff there was an underlying gentleness and appreciation in the words. Abbey was left with the feeling that Pierre Knowles would do anything for her at any time. It was more than gratitude. More than friendship. It was a strange sensation and one she'd never experienced before.

'You're part of his family now,' Joshua said after they'd transferred Pierre to the helicopter. He spoke close to her ear as the starting-up noises of the helicopter drowned out everything else. Abbey felt his warm breath fan her neck and was unable to control the shiver that passed through her. His fresh scent was teasing her senses and she wished he'd just take a bit of a step back so they weren't so close.

'His family?'

'Pierre is the type of man who only lets certain people into his inner circle.'

'Does he not have a family of his own?'

'He's married. Five grown-up children but that's not what I meant. Pierre is old school. He's the type of man who gives you his respect but only after you've earned it.'

'And I've just earned it?' Abbey's eyebrows hit her hairline in delighted surprise. Joshua tried not to let the way this gorgeous woman looked affect him. Didn't she have any idea just how sweet and lovely she looked right now, her brown hair, pulled back into a ponytail, wisps of it circling around her neck in the breeze?

'You have.' Joshua nodded. 'As far as you treating the rig staff, things will run smoothly for you. Anything you need or want, Pierre will bend over backwards to do his best to provide it.'

'Really? New laparoscope? New chair? New pair of sunglasses?' she asked quickly.

Joshua chuckled. 'Not sure about the first one but the other two sound feasible.'

'Have I earned Pierre's trust or yours?' For some reason, his answer was really important to her. Rivals they may have been but what they were doing here now in the outback wasn't medical school any more.

Joshua leaned a little closer again as he spoke. 'You've always had my trust, Abbey. Always.'

At his nearness, Abbey swallowed and tried not to look into his eyes, but it was hard not to. Breathing out slowly, she noticed that neither of them backed away, both of them caught in a time vortex, the past and the present mingling together to form something new.

'Abbey,' he breathed, and tucked a strand of hair behind her ear. Abbey's lips parted at the touch, at the way heat seemed to spread through-out her entire body as his hand came to rest on her shoulder. His gaze flicked from her eyes to her lips and back again, and she tried desperately to control herself.

It wouldn't take much, just a slight shift for-ward, a tilt of her head, to bring him closer, to let him know she was right there with him even though she had no idea exactly where she was. The helicopter, Pierre all seemed to fade into nothingness as they looked deeply into each other's eyes. He wanted to kiss her. There was no doubt about it and it appeared, from the way she wasn't pulling back from him, that she was more than happy to accept. He'd often wondered what it would be like to kiss Abbey. He'd thought about it when they'd been at med school but both of them had been far too focused on their studies to even risk it if the kiss turned out to be a nightmare.

Was it simply burning curiosity? Was it the heightened circumstances they'd found themselves in today? He'd stood in an operating theatre and he'd been able to conquer that fear because of Abbey…because of the remarkable woman who was now looking at him as though she wanted nothing more than for him to take her in his arms and plunder her mouth.

As the helicopter started to rise into the air, Joshua's insides sank. He was becoming far too attracted to her and although he kept telling himself to stop, it didn't seem to be working.

CHAPTER FIVE

ON SATURDAY, the end of her first official week working in the outback, Abbey was exhausted but thoroughly elated. After a busy week of learning the ropes, of moving from the pub into her own residence, of watching and observing not only the people she worked with but the locals who lived in town, she knew she'd made the right decision. Life here was completely different from that of a busy hospital in a bustling city but it was the type of life she'd been looking for.

Given the rushed initiation she'd had on her first day into Yawonnadeere life, on day two Joshua had declared they would take it easy. He'd shown her around the surgery, pointing out where things were in her consulting room, and then, as they'd had no patients booked for that day, they'd returned to the pub where she'd been coaxed behind the bar and taught how to pull a beer.

'All outback people know how to pull a beer,' Mark had told her as Joshua had sat on a bar stool and watched. His children had been running around the nearly deserted room, playing hide and seek amongst the chairs. Abbey had been mesmerised by them, their gorgeous innocence shining through as they'd crawled beneath the tables, the chair legs doing little to obscure them from view, and then acting all surprised whenever they'd found each other.

They were two children who really did seem to be 'owned' by the town. Now that Joshua had explained about their mother, how she'd died in childbirth, Abbey could well understand why everyone had rallied around him, helping out wherever was needed. It wouldn't have been easy, having two newborn premature babies while still trying to work and grieve for the loss of his wife. It helped her to realise just how much pain he must have faced and she started looking at him differently, watching him more closely.

On Wednesday, Joshua had taken her out to the rig again where they'd held a small clinic. The injuries had ranged from a cut finger to an ingrown toe nail to a nasty-looking rash. The afternoon had been spent with Joshua and his children, visiting other locals in town, such as the vet and the full-time police officer.

Jimmy and Becka were delightful to be around, both jabbering away to each other about their up-and-coming birthday in a language Abbey found difficult to decipher at times. However, the words 'cake' and 'presents' and 'yummy' were often quite clear.

On Thursday, Pierre had returned to the town and to his own residence not far from the rig, Joshua giving the man's wife strict instructions that he was supposed to be on bed rest for the next week at least. Pierre had harrumphed in annoyance but had promised Joshua he'd at least try to stay quiet.

Friday and Saturday had all been a mix of some-thing medical and then something social. Abbey discovered there were no real set Monday to Friday doctors' hours. They were either on duty or off duty, regardless of day or time. There were days, such as Wednesday, when they consulted at the rig and other days when they'd spend all day at the surgery, consulting and treating patients.

'It comes in waves,' he'd told her on Saturday afternoon. 'We'll have weeks where we're in the surgery consulting all week long and then times like this when it's quite dull and boring.' Patients could either make appointments or just turn up. Giselle and Mark ran a monthly immunisation clinic and as far as Abbey could see, everything was well structured and all needs were catered for. It was a strange sort of way to go on but it had apparently been working that way for the past fifty years—since Dr Turner had come to town—and that's the way it would stay.

Throughout the entire week, Joshua had been polite and professional. He'd patiently explained things to her, introduced her to people and made sure she was settling nicely into her new accommodation. In short, he'd been the perfect host and it was starting to rattle her.

Where was the Joshua who had met her off the plane? Where was the person who had challenged her and argued with her so ardently in the past? He was definitely all ease and friendliness but it somehow didn't feel right—not since they'd talked on the verandah after Pierre's operation. He'd been nothing but polite and professional.

Abbey lay in her bed, the clock telling her it was just after three o'clock on Sunday morning yet sleep was definitely somewhere else. All she could think about was Joshua and the way he'd looked at her as the helicopter had whirred noisily beside them. He'd stared at her so intently, so deeply, the touch of his hand tucking her hair behind her ear. Abbey moaned and closed her eyes, recalling exactly how he'd made her feel. Her heart pounded double time against her chest, her throat went dry, her breathing erratic, her knees weakened at his sweet touch.

She'd hoped then that he'd follow through on what she'd seen in his eyes. There had been desire, desire for her in those gorgeous blue depths of his, and she'd parted her lips, silently urging him to come closer even though she'd known it was so incredibly wrong.

'It *is* wrong,' she said out loud as she swung her legs over the side of the bed and stood up. 'You are colleagues. You have to work together until January next year. Are you a complete idiot? To want him to come near you? To hold you? To kiss you?' She walked to the mirror and stared at her reflection. 'This is Joshua we're talking about,' she told herself sternly. 'You don't even like him.'

But that was where she was wrong. She may not have liked him much back in medical school, his total obnoxiousness driving her insane, but now it was completely different. He'd been through so much, blaming himself for his wife's death, raising two children on his own, caring for the people of this town.

He was an enigma. There was no doubt about it and she had to admit she had enjoyed watching him this past week. The way he seemed to fit in perfectly with the townsfolk, the way he was attentive towards his children, the way he cared for his patients. It was all so typically Joshua but at the same time she couldn't help missing the old antagonistic Joshua.

Feeling stifled by the four walls, the ceiling fan whirring steadily above her, Abbey walked to her front door and stepped out onto the verandah. All of the houses in the main street had verandahs. They were all weatherboard, well-worn, well-loved houses and now, with the absence of any cars, any sounds in the main street of town and, thank goodness, any flies, Abbey sat down in the old rocking chair, which had come with the house.

She looked across at the surgery directly opposite her place. Joshua's house was situated at the back of the surgery and while she hadn't seen inside it, she imagined it to be as neat and as practical as her own little house. He also didn't seem to spend much time there, preferring the pub instead. With the days being so incredibly hot, it was always better for his children to be playing inside rather than risk getting sunburnt outside, their soft, young skin at risk to the elements.

This was the outback and as Abbey had read during her preliminary research, it had two seasons—wet and dry. She was actually quite pleased she'd come during the dry and could, therefore, get to know the whys and wherefores of the town without having to worry about getting flooded.

She had enough to do as it was. That included trying to figure out why Joshua seemed to be occupying so much of her thoughts. She remembered in medical school that, like her, he hadn't dated anyone, preferring to focus on his studies. They had been two workaholics, feeding off each other, determined to get the best marks, do the best research, hand in the best projects. Secretly,

she'd admired him, not only for his good looks
but also for his dedication. Of course, she would
have rather had her teeth pulled than admit it.
He'd pushed her to do her best, to work and study
hard. Now, though, if the few strange and electrifying moments they'd shared were anything to
go on, they appeared more than happy to study
each other rather than medicine. Did he feel that
same tug of awareness she did whenever they
were alone together?

'You're being ridiculous,' she told herself
softly, shaking her head. The poor man was obviously still traumatised from his wife's death.
He wouldn't want to get involved with anyone
and he surely wouldn't want her when he discovered her secret. No man ever would. Abbey took
a deep breath. But that didn't matter any more.
She didn't need anyone, any man, to be who she
was deep down inside. She was alive, and that
was enough to be grateful for. She had to keep
remembering that.

It was so silly that for the past sixteen years

since medical school, she hadn't cared one iota where he was or what he'd been doing, hadn't even thought of him. Obviously he'd met a woman and married before tragedy had struck his life. At least he'd had the opportunity to have such a life. Abbey had long since regretted her decision to focus on her career, desperate to advance in the medical field and succeed with honours.

Well, she'd done all of that and not needed someone special in her life, someone to share the highs and the lows, to help when things didn't go exactly according to plan. Someone to come home to at the end of the day. Someone to share her most private, most intimate thoughts with. Someone to just sit and be with her. Someone like Joshua.

He'd suffered a great loss, though, and that could take a while to get over. She understood that. She knew the way emotions could rise up and overwhelm, how irrationality could make a person do things they wouldn't normally do, how lonely walking through the valley of despair could really be.

As she sat there dressed in her summer pyjamas—pink with red hearts—quietly rocking and thinking, a light went on in the surgery.

Abbey instantly stopped rocking and sat forward in the chair, her heart starting to beat wildly against her chest. Had someone broken into the surgery? There were plenty of drugs stored there and she'd been more than relieved to find Joshua kept them locked as tight as a drum. He might leave his car keys in his car at all times, the doors to his house might be unlocked, but the medication and patient files were kept firmly under lock and key.

She stood up, wondering if she should go and investigate further. Should she go and wake Wally, the town's police officer? Should she creep around the back of the surgery to Joshua's place and wake him instead?

Indecision warred within her but just as she stood, deciding to at least go over and take a closer look, the front door to the surgery opened and out walked Joshua, barefoot, dressed only in denim jeans, something dark bundled in his arms.

Abbey paused at the top leading to her house and looked across at him. Obviously, he was no criminal come to steal the drugs from the surgery, so why had her heart started pounding even louder than before? What was he doing? Perhaps it was best she didn't know because, dressed as he was, his chest bare and enticing, she might not be able to resist the urge to run her fingers through the crinkly hairs that dusted his skin.

She was about to turn and head back inside when he looked over and saw her standing there.

'Abbey?'

'Hi.' There were a few streetlights on in the town but most of the light was coming from his house, meaning she could make out every contour of his gorgeous body. Her breathing started to increase and again she knew she should just say goodnight, turn and go inside, yet she felt like a cane toad caught in the headlights—stunned and unable to move.

He put down the bundle of whatever it was he'd been holding and headed across the road, not even bothering to check for any cars. 'Is everything all right? What's wrong?' He walked from the light into the darkness surrounding her house and while she may not have been able to see him as clearly as before, she could feel him instead. He stopped at her bottom step, looking at her, concern etched into his brow.

'I'm fine. Just…you know…couldn't sleep.'

'I guess the heat does take a while to get used to,' he said, his voice soft and calm.

The heat had nothing to do with it and she knew herself to be a liar as she simply nodded her head, letting him think what he wanted. There was no way she was telling him the truth, no way she was letting him know that it was thoughts of him that were keeping her awake. Now, with him standing there before her, so scantily clad, it was only making matters worse. Now she had a dry mouth as well, and knew she'd never get back to sleep.

He ran a hand through his hair, mussing it up, which only added to his appeal. Abbey swallowed a few times, stretching out her hand to the verandah post beside her for support. Why did he have to look so incredible? Why did he have to be so sweetly concerned for her? Why had he been awake at three o'clock in the morning?

'Everything all right with you?' she asked.

'Yeah. Too much to do.' He wasn't going to tell her that he couldn't sleep either, and that it had nothing at all to do with the heat. He'd been thinking of her, of how well she'd fitted into the routine of the town, how well liked she was, how well *he* was coming to like her and how fighting the attraction he felt towards her was becoming increasingly difficult with each passing day.

One week. She'd been back in his life for one week and after that first electrifying day he'd decided it would be best to pull right back and to treat her merely as another colleague. Now, looking at her standing on the step, dressed in cotton pyjamas consisting of a top with thin little straps and a pair of low-hung trousers, it was all he could do to keep his tongue from rolling out of his mouth and hitting the ground. Her hair was down, floating around her perfect shoulders, thankfully hiding her glorious neck, which he'd had visions of nuzzling. She looked incredible and the fact that they were the same age only impressed him even more.

What he wanted to do was to close the distance between them, to take her in his arms, to press his mouth to hers, to feel her skin beneath his hands, to explore the contours of her luscious body and to never stop.

What he *did* was to take a step back towards the road. 'I've uh…just got to…um…' He closed his eyes for a second, trying to get his thoughts back on track. 'Hang twinkle lights.'

Abbey tilted her head to the side, unsure she'd heard him correctly. 'You're hanging twinkle lights at three o'clock in the morning?'

'If you can think of another way to turn my home into a magical fairyland, then tell me.'

She laughed, realising the request must have come from the twins. 'Just as well they didn't want you to make it into a gingerbread house.'

'I didn't even think of that,' he groaned. 'Wouldn't that have been a nightmare?' He glanced at her then joined in with her laughter, the tense atmosphere of a moment ago starting to dissipate.

'Want some help?' she found herself asking, and could have bitten her tongue the instant the words were out.

'Are you sure?' He wasn't too sure himself. Being so close to her, hanging twinkle lights together, when the one thing he'd been trying to do all week long was keep his distance.

'It makes sense, Joshua. We're both wide awake. You'll get the lights sorted out and put up faster if there are two of us doing it and then you can move on to the next thing on your list. I've never planned a three-year-old's birthday party before but I'm sure you have more things to get done before they both wake up at the first sign of light.'

'You are so right. When both of them open their eyes, it's as though the "on" switch has been flicked and all of their energy for the day comes flooding through them. When they're awake, they're *awake*.'

'Right. Then let's get these lights hung.' She would concentrate on helping him. She would be a good neighbour, helping out a friend. That was all. She wouldn't look at his firm, muscled chest. Neither would she admire how his well-worn denims had long forgotten any shape but his own. She was a doctor and she'd seen plenty of naked bodies before now without the slightest reaction. That's how she would deal with being so close to him while they did this simple task—in a professional, anatomical way.

As they walked across the street, she focused on where she put her bare feet, not used to being shoeless.

'It won't take too long,' he told her. 'I've strung lights around the house before so there are nails and clips in place, ready to help and to hold.'

'Excellent.' As they walked into the light she began to wonder whether she was going to be able to keep herself under control. In the dark, she hadn't been able to clearly see the defined muscles, the way a smattering of brown hair caressed his skin, the way the sturdy material pulled across his butt as he bent to pick up the ladder he'd obviously brought out earlier. She swallowed over her suddenly dry throat and when he turned to look at her, she quickly raised her eyes to meet his, forcing a smile. 'Ready?'

'Yes.' He positioned the ladder. He thought he'd felt her gaze on him but had been in the process of telling himself not to be such a fool when he'd turned and caught her checking him out. He swallowed a quick laugh then climbed up the ladder, steadying himself with one hand against the house guttering and pointed down to the lights. 'They're coiled in a way that if you just hand me the top end, and hold them loosely with your arm through the middle, it should unravel quite easily without tangling.'

He watched as she bent and picked up the lights, finding the end. She looked even more like a pint-sized dynamo but a softer one in the pink girly pyjamas. He hadn't pegged her for a pink sort of girl. Becka most certainly was but, then, his daughter was all about frills and lace. The more the better. Perhaps, because his earlier relationship with Abbey had been more antagonistic, he'd always thought of her more as a prickly echidna rather than anything girly. Now, though, she looked soft and sweet and incredibly sexy. He swallowed, telling himself to concentrate or he'd probably end up falling off the ladder.

Together, they both managed to control their wayward thoughts and soon the lights were strung. 'Let me give them a test,' he said, and quickly went inside. Abbey stepped back into the middle of the road and watched as first the surgery went dark and then in another moment the front of his house was indeed lit up like a magical fairyland.

'Wow,' she breathed as Joshua came out to stand next to her. 'It's gorgeous.' She glanced up at him. 'Joshua, they're going to love it. You're a good dad.'

'Well…' He shrugged and she realised he felt uncomfortable with the compliment.

'You're up at such a ridiculous hour, creating a fairyland for them, making sure they have a wonderful birthday.' Did being busy, doing things like this also help him to forget the anniversary of his wife's death? Was that why he couldn't sleep? Again Abbey was struck with the impression that he was too hard on himself, that he needed to let go of his past and move forward into his future rather than blaming himself for what had happened to his wife. Although he'd told her that he'd *killed* his wife, she was positive that wasn't really the case. He perhaps had been unable to *save* her but not the other. Yet she also knew that over-achievers, such as they were, often blamed themselves far too deeply and for far too long.

'And that reminds me that I still have quite a few more things to get done.' Things that wouldn't get done if he continued to stand in the middle of the main street alongside his enticing colleague at half past three in the morning.

'Right. Sure.'

Why did she sound so disappointed? Did she want to keep hanging out with him? Working methodically through his list?

She jerked her thumb over her shoulder. 'I might go have a cup of herbal tea. See if that won't help me get back to sleep.'

'You have herbal teas?'

Abbey was surprised. 'I do. I brought them with me. They help me unwind.'

'Me too.' And he was currently out of his own personal stock and the pub most certainly didn't offer herbal teas on their menu.

'Do…you…want to join me for a quick cuppa?'

'We could sit out on your verandah and admire the twinkle lights,' he ventured, not wanting to set foot inside her house because if he did, he might well be tempted to forget the list he had to get through before his kids woke up.

'OK. I'll go and put the kettle on.'

'I'll pack up the ladder.'

Abbey tried not to hug herself close, tried to contain the excitement she felt at getting to spend some personal time like this with Joshua.

'Uh…what sort would you like? I have peppermint, chamomile, ginger and rhubarb.'

'Rhubarb? Seriously?'

'Absolutely.'

'Then I'll have to go with the rhubarb. Thanks.' His smile was one that caused her entire body to flood with tingles and anticipatory delight.

'OK. I'll see you in a bit.'

'Good-o.'

They both went their separate ways, intent on doing what needed to be done so they could come back together and just be.

When Abbey carried two mugs of tea to the verandah, she was surprised to find him already sitting down. He'd obviously brought the chair over from his own place as she only had the one rocking chair available. He'd also put on a T-shirt and for that she was very thankful. It would be much easier to keep her distance from him when she wasn't itching to touch his gorgeous body.

'Here you go. I haven't sugared it.'

'I don't take sugar,' he told her, accepting the cup with a murmur of thanks. Abbey sat in the rocking chair and sipped her tea, both of them looking at the lights.

'They look so pretty.'

'Not a bad job,' he agreed.

'The twins will love it.'

'Yes they will.' He thought about how his children would react when the sun went down tomorrow night, how delighted they'd be to see their house twinkle like a fairyland. He loved them a lot but some days he had no idea how to show them how much he really cared. He could provide for them, that's what parents did. He could do practical things such as putting up lights or painting their latest favourite cartoon character on their bedroom walls, yet he couldn't help feeling that he didn't deserve the love and kisses they would often shower him with given that he was responsible for them losing their mother.

'You're a good dad,' she said again.

'Some may disagree with you.'

'Who?'

'Their mother.'

'I don't think so, Joshua.'

'Miriam hated the outback. She didn't want the children raised in some out-of-the-way backwater, as she termed it.'

The way he spoke of his wife, his words carrying a hint of bitterness, struck Abbey with the thought that perhaps his marriage hadn't been as happy as she'd originally thought. 'You've obviously done what was best for the twins. Everyone in this town loves them to pieces. They bring so much happiness and joy to everyone they meet.

I've been watching them and seeing the reactions in others.'

'I guess we all have our own reasons for coming out into the middle of nowhere. Kids or no kids.' He paused and sipped his tea, unable to look at the woman beside him as the rocking chair moved back and forth over the boards. 'We're all hiding from something.'

'Perhaps we're running towards it?' she offered.

'What about you, Abbey? What made you sign up with PMA?' He watched her closely for a moment. The way his blue eyes seemed to be able to look right through her made Abbey want to squirm on her seat but instead she calmly raised her tea cup to her lips and took a sip.

'I'm trying to find my life.'

He raised his eyebrows. 'Why? Love life gone bad? Trying to figure out who you are?' He knew that feeling all too well, especially as after three years he still had no idea how to be a single father. He was an academic, someone who preferred to search for the answers to questions in a book or to dissect something in order to discover the answer. Learning on the job had been tough enough in the medical world but it was nowhere near as difficult as the world of single parenting. 'What happened to make you want a different life?'

'I was forced into a different life, Joshua. One I most certainly didn't ask for but one which has made me completely re-evaluate everything,' she said softly, but there was bitterness and anger in her words.

'Cancer?'

'Good guess.'

'It's an easy guess nowadays, unfortunately. Cancer now affects one in every two people.'

'Sad but true,' she replied.

'I'm also guessing that due to the protective shell you have wrapped firmly around you, the cancer struck you, rather than a loved one.'

'Right again. You always were a good psych.' She drank the rest of her tea, barely tasting it, and put her cup down on the floor.

Abbey had had cancer? He felt the enormity of the situation and as he was a doctor, he also knew how it would have affected her life. Although there had been times in their past when they had argued and annoyed each other until both of them had wanted to scream, he'd never wanted anything bad to happen to her. It disturbed him greatly that it had.

'Are you OK now?' Joshua's words were gentle and it was that tone, that caring, sweet tone that made tears spring unbidden to Abbey's eyes. 'Oh, gosh. You're not.' Before he knew what he was doing, he placed his hand over hers and held her hand tightly. 'Abbey. Tell me you're OK.' For some strange reason, he desperately needed to hear her say she was all right. He'd hoped that during her time here that they could become friends but as he touched her now, as he waited while she struggled to pull herself together, he realised he already felt more than friendship for her.

Why was he being so sweet? So caring? It only

made her emotions more intense. The tears started to fall and she wiped them away with her free hand, working hard to ignore the way the warmth from his touch was making her tremble.

'Technically,' she said after sniffing a few times, 'I'm fine.'

He breathed out, releasing some of the tension he'd felt, but his concern for her was still uppermost in his mind. 'But emotionally?'

'Emotionally?' Abbey swallowed over the lump in her throat and tried not to hiccup. 'I'll never be the same. I'll never be the same woman I was before I had cancer. My life was torn apart, torn into shreds, and it feels as though I'll never be able to piece it back together. I try. I've been trying so hard to get some sort of control over my life, to find out where I fit into the grand scheme of things now that this has happened to me, but I don't know…' She hiccuped again. 'I don't know if I ever will.'

'Abbey.' Her name was wrenched from his lips

with a thread of pain. He hated seeing her like this. 'What sort of cancer did you have?'

She looked at him, her brown eyes filled with pain and utter desolation as she said one word. 'Ovarian.' Her bottom lip started to quiver and she gripped his hand tightly, needing to draw strength from him. She hiccuped again, knowing she must look a ghastly sight but not caring any more. 'I'll never…' She swallowed and shook her head before saying quickly, 'I'll never be able to have children. I'll never be a mother.' With that, she pulled her hand from his and covered her face, sobs racking her body.

CHAPTER SIX

JOSHUA was stunned.

She'd had ovarian cancer and as she'd told him that she could never have children, he could only surmise that the surgeon would have taken all her reproductive organs rather than risk the cancer spreading.

Her hair was shoulder length but it was shiny and rich in its vibrant chocolaty-brown colour. Had she lost her hair? Needed chemotherapy? Were there any secondaries? Was she really OK? His heart clenched with fear at the thought.

As she sat there and cried, struggling to get herself under control, Joshua was conflicted about what to do. He quickly pulled a clean handkerchief from his pocket and held it out to her.

'Here,' he offered, and she took it with gratitude. He was itching to pull her close to him so she could cry her pain out but he wasn't sure that would be such a good idea. After the moment they'd shared at the helicopter, he knew keeping his distance was of paramount importance. They were friends and that's the way it had to stay.

He sat there, feeling strange and self-conscious and guilty. He hadn't expected the last emotion and he frowned. Yes, it was definitely guilt and he wondered at it. Was he feeling guilty because he'd been given two incredible children at the expense of their mother's life? Here Abbey was, sitting before him, wiping her eyes, blowing her nose in an effort to get herself back under control because she'd just confessed a very important and emotional secret to him—she couldn't have children. Of course, a declaration like that would bring his own children to mind, children who had wrapped their arms around his neck less than a few hours ago, giving him wet and sloppy kisses as he'd tucked them into bed.

'Sorry,' she mumbled, and forced a smile.

'No, no. Don't you dare apologise.' He was quick to reassure her.

'I don't usually break down and cry like that.'

'Hey, it's me, Abbey. Good ol' Joshua, and, besides, you've no doubt had an emotionally draining week, coming to a new place, being faced with new experiences and trying to gain some control over your immediate circumstances.' He remembered the way they'd argued when she'd got off the plane and he felt bad. Still, he couldn't go back and change things. That was definitely a lesson he'd learned the hard way. 'So where you would normally have had some reserves to help you keep your feelings in check, those reserves have all been used up in coming here to Yawonnadeere Creek.'

'Hmm. Well, when you put it like that…' She trailed off and laughed a little.

'The last thing you need to be doing right now is beating yourself up because your tears overflowed.' His words were deep and soothing and Abbey thought she'd be able to listen to that gorgeous voice of his all day long. 'We all have bad days.'

'Yes. You're right. We do. I'll just chalk this up to a necessary release of emotions and then I can move on.'

'That's more like it. Positive thoughts.'

'You could do with some yourself.'

'What?' Joshua was momentarily taken aback.

'You still blame yourself for your wife's death.'

He looked away for the moment, unable to believe she could read him so easily. Was it the fact that they'd known each other all those years ago or was he that transparent? As everyone in the town had been around when Miriam had gone into labour, they knew the story. He knew no one blamed him for her death, that he'd done everything he could to save his wife but it just hadn't been enough. With Abbey being an outsider, with him telling her about his past, about what had happened to the twins' mother, she was bound to see things differently.

'You didn't *kill* her. I'll bet if I looked at the operation report for your wife, it would show that you made no errors, that you did everything you possibly could, but things just hadn't turned out the way you'd planned. I'm positive it wasn't your fault.'

Joshua clenched his jaw, not sure how they'd managed to work their way around to this topic but here they were. 'Knowing the truth and mentally accepting it are two different things.'

'So you're telling me that you know you didn't actually *kill* your wife.' She spoke the words softly, pleased he hadn't bitten her head off or told her to drop the subject.

'It feels like it. I had the skill. I had the knowledge.' He shook his head. 'I should have sent her back to Adelaide sooner rather than later.'

'But you didn't.'

'No. We'd come here for a six-month rotation, just like you, sent here with PMA.'

'She was a doctor?'

'Yes.' Joshua put his cup down on the ground

and stood, his shoulders tense as the memories came back. 'She wasn't working when she came here. Perhaps that was part of the problem but she'd taken time off work because of the pregnancy, which meant she was here as a spouse rather than a doctor.'

'That couldn't have been easy for her.'

'It wasn't. She'd been fine in the beginning, telling me to get the rotation here out of the way sooner rather than later.'

Abbey frowned at that. 'It sounds as though she didn't enjoy it here.'

'She didn't. She was pregnant with twins.' Twins she didn't want, he added silently. 'And the heat wasn't good for her.'

'Hence ending up with pre-eclampsia.'

'Dr Turner and I were monitoring her closely, making sure she was all right, and she was. She was doing great and then just like that...' He snapped his fingers '...things went bad. Pre-eclampsia turned into eclampsia and even though I delivered the twins, even though I did everything I could, I couldn't save her.' He shook his head. Shame, mortification and guilt—his close associates these past three years—swamped him again. 'As a result of my failure to save my wife, every time I stand next to an operating table all I can see is her limp, lifeless body, lying there.' He kept his back to Abbey, his words vehement and laced with pain.

'No wonder you went so pale.'

He snorted with derision. 'Today. Today is the anniversary of Miriam's death and she's still making me feel guilty for what happened.'

'Or perhaps you don't feel as though you have a right to be happy?' she tried. 'You didn't kill Miriam.'

'I didn't save her either.' He hadn't spoken about Miriam to anyone in a very long time. 'I keep thinking, if only I'd realised sooner what was going to happen. If only I'd sent her back to Adelaide where she would have had trained staff and equipment to help her.'

'You can't play the "what if" game. Do you

know what I've discovered, Joshua? It never ends the way you want it to. You can play one scenario after another over and over in your mind but it doesn't work. You know, uh…what if we hadn't taken that particular flight, or what if we'd left on a different day, or what if I'd recognised the symptoms earlier? Everyone does it.' Abbey shook her head sadly. 'Reality always comes back to bite you.'

He glanced over at her for a moment and realised that she understood. Their worlds had been blown apart, for completely different reasons but, still, blown right apart. 'After three years, Abbey, I still feel as though I'm floundering in a sea of confusion, still trying to pick up the pieces of my past life and fit them back together.'

'Only it doesn't work any more, does it?' She nodded. 'The pieces that used to slot in perfectly together don't fit any more.'

'Yes.' He turned to look at her.

'That's because they're not the pieces of your *new* life.' She looked away from him as she spoke, still feeling vulnerable from her previous outburst of tears. 'I can never physically carry a child within me. That is an absolute fact. Nothing in this world is going to change that.'

'There are other ways for you to be a mother, though,' he pointed out.

'Exactly. The pieces of my life have been changed. Your wife died. That's an absolute fact but you have two gorgeous children who adore you and a town that has accepted you.'

'My pieces have changed.' He said the words softly and nodded. 'Now, *that* makes perfect sense to me.'

'Good.'

'I think you always aced me in psych,' he said, and Abbey couldn't help but smile. 'There's no way I would have admitted it back then but I don't think I would have scored as well as I did if we hadn't had that rivalry in place.'

'Agreed. We fed off each other, both determined, both wanting to be the best.'

'Both equally pig-headed.'

Abbey laughed and leaned further back into the rocking chair. 'Those were the days.'

'Why do they seem so simple now?' He smiled, stretching his arms above his head, working out the kinks in his muscles. Abbey's eyes almost bugged out of her head as his jeans dipped a little and his untucked shirt rose. Although he'd been walking around before with no shirt on at all, the small glimpse she now had of his lower abdomen brought back all the feelings she had just managed to get under some level of control.

He angled his head from side to side, carefully stretching his neck, and then raked his fingers through his hair, giving it a little massage. Abbey licked her lips and slowly exhaled the breath she hadn't realised she'd been holding.

The man was completely gorgeous. How could any woman not be affected by him? How could *she* not be affected by him? By the way his blue come-hither eyes made her feel, by the way his rich voice washed over her and reduced her body to a mass of tingles? Thank goodness he'd closed his eyes when he'd started stretching because she was having one heck of a difficult time looking away.

Never had a man made her feel so conscious of her femininity as Joshua Ackles did. That was the way it had always been but now, all these years later with all of their training and mistakes behind them, there was definitely something brewing between them. Abbey wasn't sure what it was or what she was supposed to do about it, but she'd discovered so much about him—about the *real* him—and she felt privileged that he'd opened up to her.

Perhaps that was why she'd felt comfortable sharing her own tragedy with him. She knew he wouldn't tell anyone, that she could trust him with her deepest secrets, but even now as she forced herself to look away, to make sure he didn't catch her ogling his sublime body, she also recognised that she'd opened up to him because she felt comfortable talking to him. Whatever had existed between them all those years ago, that spark of desire, that spark of trust, that spark of repressed need…it was still there and it was growing with each passing second they spent in each other's company.

When he looked at her again, she hoped the slight tinge of pink on her cheeks wasn't as noticeable as it felt because from her standpoint she was burning up with embarrassment at her uncontrollable reaction to him.

'Well…uh…I'd better go,' he said.

'Ah, yes. The list of things still to be done.'

'Thanks for the tea.' He hadn't moved, was still leaning against her rail, not too far from where she sat. Abbey curled her legs beneath her, trying to keep herself in check given that the urge to stand, to step forward and throw herself into his arms was becoming rather difficult to resist.

'My pleasure.'

Joshua stood there, arms folded over his chest as he watched her in the rocking chair. She'd tucked her legs up beneath her, as though to protect herself. Her eyes were telling him to come closer, to take this strange awareness they had of each other to the next level, but her body language was telling him a different story.

His own body was still warm from the visual caress she'd given him. He'd stretched, his muscles tired and aching, and when he'd opened his eyes, looking at her through hooded lashes, he'd realised she was checking him out. Joshua had been unable to stop the spread of typical male pride at the realisation that a stunningly beautiful and highly intelligent woman, such as Abbey Bateman, found him attractive.

It was almost like the perfect beginning to an otherwise draining day. 'Thanks, Abbey.'

'For?' She couldn't take her eyes off him. She wanted him to step forward to take her in his arms, to press his mouth to hers, to soothe the burning sensation still thrumming through her after she'd watched him stretch.

'For, uh…getting me to talk. I didn't like it but…I think I needed it.'

She nodded slowly, her breathing becoming

more difficult to control every moment he stayed where he was. He'd said he was going to go, but the longer he didn't move, the harder it was for her to stay where she was. 'Me too. Thanks for listening and also for not hugging me when I started crying. If you had, I would still be here weeping in your arms and no doubt soaking your shirt.'

'I doubt any man would complain about a soaked shirt if he was holding a gorgeous woman in his arms.' His tone was deep, vibrating through her. 'I can think of worse ways to spend my time.'

Abbey's throat went dry again. Had Joshua just called her gorgeous? The tingles, the blush, the flutterings. They all started up again and she knew he had to go sooner rather than later. Joshua Ackles was starting to become too tempting and she hadn't come here to be tempted. And she was sure he was flirting with her.

'Oh?' She licked her lips, unable to look away from him.

'Abbey,' he groaned as though he was in pain. 'Don't look at me like that.'

'Like what?'

'Like you want me to scoop you up and carry you inside.'

She gasped at his words, astounded he could read her so easily. 'Inside?' She shook her head. 'No. You and me, inside the house. Alone. No. We can't.' Her eyes were wide, filled with a mixture of curiosity and logic.

'Then stop looking at me like that.' He rolled his eyes, mad at himself for not being able to control his desire for her and mad at her for looking so adorable that he desired her in the first place. 'I don't understand why it's so difficult this time around.'

'What's difficult? What do you mean?' Abbey stopped rocking and put her feet on the decking.

'You.'

'I'm difficult? *I'm* not the one who's being difficult, Joshua.'

'No. You're being wonderful and adorable and all sexy sitting there in the rocking chair, tucking your feet beneath you and just…looking…' He stopped and closed his eyes. 'I used to be able to control the way you made me feel. Back in medical school, you used to look at me with those big brown eyes of yours and I'd end up being a slobbering mess, unable to remember what my name was. That's why I couldn't work with you when we were thrust together as lab partners. That was why I used to annoy you so much, because I couldn't handle the way you used to make me feel. I nearly flunked my last exam because just before we went in, you came up to me and batted your eyelashes at me and said in your most facetious tone, "Good luck, Joshua. You're going to need it."'

'That's hardly fair. You can't go blaming me for you nearly flunking an exam.'

'You knew back then that you could rile me.'

'Just as you used to rile me.' She stood and crossed her arms over her chest. 'You used to unnerve me just as much back then as you do now, Joshua Ackles, so don't go blaming me because you're unable to control this frightening natural chemistry that seems to exist between us.'

He stepped forward. 'I didn't ask for it. Not back then. Not now.'

Abbey stepped forward too, bringing them toe to toe, her hands now dropping to her sides as she clenched them into fists, still astounded that the man could make her so mad. 'Neither. Did. I.'

They were close now. So close she could feel his breath on her face. Their scents mixed and mingled, drawing them closer.

'Argh. You are the most frustrating woman I've ever met!' His gaze dipped down to her mouth then back to her eyes again as he worked hard at controlling himself. Only Abbey had ever affected him this way and he was through struggling against it.

'*I'm* frustrating? That's just plain ridicul—'

Joshua had had enough. He grabbed her by the shoulders and hauled her close before shutting her up by clamping his mouth firmly over hers.

CHAPTER SEVEN

HIS mouth on hers. He wasn't the least bit hesitant as he channelled sixteen years of repression into that kiss. It was powerful, hungry and full of heat.

He wanted her. That much was absolutely clear and Abbey couldn't believe how incredible even that small smidgen of knowledge felt. Of course, there was the fact that Joshua was kissing her. Her mind was sluggish as it processed the information. The man who had given her so much grief in medical school, who had often driven her to distraction with his gibes and questions, had been yearning for her. Abbey was equally as slow in realising that she'd been yearning just as much for him. Secretly, she knew she'd known it all along, as had he but lying to themselves had been necessary in order to keep their focus on their studies.

Not so now.

Their breathing synchronised as they allowed themselves to be swept away with the powerful drive that encompassed them. It was glorious that after so many years of denying himself the right to feel these emotions, he could now touch her. She was letting him in, allowing him into her life in a way he had never thought possible, and again the need to thank her swelled within him. He so desperately wanted to stay here, to just lock the two of them away in this moment in time. There hadn't been too many perfect moments in his life in the past few years but this was one that gave him hope—hope that there might be more than where he'd been.

For even as he allowed himself these moments, holding Abbey in his arms, her mouth responding to his with such ardent urgency, Joshua also knew nothing could ever come of the powerful need raging between them. He'd failed one woman before and he wasn't about to repeat past mistakes, especially not with a woman he respected as much as Abbey.

He shut off his mind and decided to simply concentrate on her, on holding her, touching her, kissing her. There was an uncontrollable need powering through them both, as though they had been denying themselves any emotional contact for far too long and now that things had built to a frenzy, they'd been unable to quell it. Years of repressed desire was starting to flow from both of them and neither of them wanted to stop.

He slid his hands from her shoulders down her back in order to bring her closer to him. Abbey moaned with delight, showing him that she was right there alongside him, making the journey of discovery together. Her hands had been balled into fists at her sides but now they were at his waist, her fingers sliding just beneath his T-shirt in order to feel that firm, muscled physique he'd been teasing her with earlier.

The muscles that her fingers had itched to

touch when she'd helped him hang the fairy lights were now hers to caress, to memorise, to simply enjoy. There was no denying that the man was in good shape and now the smooth contours of his back were next on her exploration list.

He continued to kiss her with passion and skill, bringing forth a response even she hadn't been aware she possessed. Here was a man who was kissing her, wanting her, making her feel more like a woman than she'd felt since before her diagnosis.

Just the thought that she was being kissed was enough to make her quiver, the action prompting Joshua to lean back against the rail, bringing her with him. He found her attractive, gorgeous, appealing. He'd called her beautiful and was kissing her like she'd never been kissed before, so rich, so desperate, so powerful. His mouth was still warm on hers, their hunger mounting together as they continued to deepen the kiss, matching each other with each mounting emotion, ensuring they took this journey of exploration together.

After a short while, Joshua broke his mouth free from hers, pressing kisses around to her ear and then down to her neck where he nuzzled in close, spreading fire-kisses onto the smooth skin. He'd fantasised about kissing her glorious neck, of feeling the silky strands of her hair between his fingers, and now he realised that his fantasies were nothing compared to the real thing, the real Abigail. Exhaling harshly, he allowed his hands to caress her back, wanting desperately to slip beneath her top, to feel her warm skin against his, but he was having a difficult time keeping himself under control at the moment. Deepening the touch would only result in him losing complete control.

'Well, that's one way to stop an argument,' she murmured as she rested her head on his chest. Joshua chuckled then brought his hands back to her shoulders, easing her back. Remorse and regret at what he'd done was starting to swamp him and even though he wanted to keep holding her, keep kissing her and nuzzling her neck, he knew he shouldn't.

There could be nothing between them except being colleagues, possibly even friends, but nothing more. He'd failed in one marriage before and now, on the third anniversary of his wife's death, here he was, kissing another woman. What Abbey had said earlier about realising the pieces of his life puzzle had changed had really resonated with him. What he needed to figure out was which pieces had changed and how he could make them fit seamlessly into his life. Kissing her, although absolutely delightful, wasn't the way to figure that out.

'Abbey?'

'Mmm?'

'I need to get going.'

Her answer was to sigh dreamily against him. It made him wonder if she'd read more into the kiss than he'd intended. He wasn't even sure that *he* knew what he'd initially intended when he'd broken through his restraint and hauled her against him, plundering her mouth as he'd been wanting to do for such an incredibly long time. Now, though, he needed to focus, to bring them out of the clouds and back down to earth and reality.

'It's after four and there are still so many things I need to get done.'

'Don't forget to try and get some sleep,' she said, pulling back, feeling slightly bereft when his hands slid from her shoulders. 'Doctor's orders,' she joked, trying to inject a bit of light-heartedness into the situation. To say she felt more confused and bewildered than before was an understatement. Joshua had kissed her, passionately kissed her, making her feel whole again for the first time since her surgery, making her feel as though she really was a woman a man could desire.

'Right. Sleep. I'll add it to my list.' He side-stepped her and headed down the stairs. 'See you later on today. Party starts in the pub at two o'clock in the afternoon,' he called as he crossed the road, then waved before he disappeared into the magical fairyland house.

Abbey stood where she was for a moment, amazed at how quick his exit had been. She touched her fingers to her lips, wondering for a split second whether she'd imagined everything. Had he been here? Had they drunk tea together? Had they kissed? The only thing which stood as testimony that she wasn't lying in her bed dreaming were the twinkling lights on the house across the street.

'Not a dream,' she muttered as she collected the cups and headed into the house. 'Dreams usually end far more happily than this.'

Abbey tossed and turned after she went back to bed, her thoughts filled to overflowing with images of Joshua. Finally, she was able to slip into a deep slumber after the sun was up. When she woke, she was astonished and embarrassed to find it was half past one in the afternoon! What must everyone think of her? The new doctor. Sleeping her Sunday away.

As she quickly showered and dressed, she realised that if her medical services had been required, someone would have come over and woken her up. The fact that they hadn't went a little way to alleviate her guilt. The twins' party was due to start soon and she still had to wrap their presents.

Rushing around, she was eventually ready. She'd pushed all thoughts of Joshua to the back of her mind, intent on finding out how he handled seeing her again. Would he be happy to see her? Would he treat her as though nothing had happened? Would he welcome her with open arms, dipping her over his arm in a tango move and then kissing her in front of everyone?

Her cheeks warmed at the thought.

Hurrying so as not to be late, Abbey grabbed her hat before heading out of the door and across the street to the pub. As she walked in, her gaze automatically sought out Joshua and she found him standing behind the bar, cocktail shaker in hand as he smiled at something Mark had said.

Rach was sitting on the floor with the twins, who were busy throwing wrapping paper around the place, enjoying themselves thoroughly. Dustin was sticking a 'pin the tail on the donkey' game to the wall and Giselle was carefully carrying a large birthday cake of the twins' favourite cartoon character to its pride of place on a table set up in the corner of the room.

'Ooh.' Becka was the first one to spot the cake. 'Look, Jimmy.'

'Ooh.' Jimmy echoed his sister, the twins standing in awe of the cake before the moment of surprise quickly passed, both of them jumping up and down and clapping with delight. 'I want some *now*.' Jimmy's declaration was met with a resounding echo of the same from his sister. It was then that Becka spied Abbey in the doorway and ran over to her, holding out her hands.

'Presents?'

Abbey smiled and bent down. 'Yes, sweetheart. This is for you.'

'And me?' Jimmy wasn't about to be outdone by his sister.

'Of course.' Abbey handed them the carefully wrapped presents, knowing that within a matter of seconds the paper would be discarded on the floor in a complete mess. 'Happy birthday.'

'What do you both say?' their father's voice reminded them, and Abbey looked up, surprised to see Joshua standing before her. She hadn't realised he'd moved.

As she slowly rose again, the twins said in unison, 'Fank you, Abbey.'

'You're welcome.' Abbey smiled as the children ripped open the paper, ooh-ing and ahh-ing as they pulled out hand-painted pictures of their favourite cartoon character. The difference with these pictures was that Abbey had captured each twin's likeness and included them in the drawing. 'You can hang them in your room,' she told the twins.

'Abbey.' Joshua was stunned, trying to get a good look at what she'd drawn. 'They're…perfect.' He turned back to look at her. 'I had no idea you could draw so incredibly well. You could do your own art show.'

She laughed at this. 'I doubt it but thank you.'

Joshua looked from the pictures, which his children were now running around showing everyone else, back to Abbey. Somewhere between the hours of decorating the house with balloons and streamers and catching a full twenty minutes worth of sleep before the twins had woken up, he'd vowed to keep his distance from Abbey. Now, as he stood there, drinking in her essence and once more being astounded by her grace and poise, he found himself failing.

What was it about this woman that made it so difficult for him to remain aloof? She took off her hat and headed further into the room, going over to give Dustin a hand as he finished organising all the 'tails' for the donkey game.

'You are looking more and more at the beautiful doctor,' Giselle murmured, coming up behind Joshua.

'Huh? What? No. We're just friends, Giselle.'

'I am French. Please do not insult my intelligence where *le langage de l'amour* is concerned.'

'I'm not trying to insult you, Giselle. It's just that Abbey and I are friends. That's all.'

Giselle huffed at his words. 'You have a chance at happiness, not like you think you had before but real happiness. Happiness like I have with my Markey. You were not happy before. It was sad, what happened to your Miriam, but that is gone now. Moving on is good.'

'Giselle,' Joshua warned, and his friend held up both of her hands in surrender.

'Australian men are all stubborn. I forget. *Pardonnez-moi, chéri.*'

More people started to arrive then and the twins were once again the centre of attention, Joshua making sure they remembered their manners as they received their gifts. Within a few hours, the

pub was filled with adults and children, the children heading into a room in the back which had
originally been the 'ladies' room' in years gone
by. Mark and Giselle had been helping Dustin and
Rach to prepare a feast for all and when the sun
started to set just after they'd all eaten, everyone
trooped outside to look at the fairyland house
Joshua had made for his children.

Throughout the afternoon and into the early
evening, Jimmy had taken an incredible shine
to her so when they headed outside, Jimmy was
firmly settled in Abbey's arms and Becka was
snuggled close to her father. This forced Abbey
and Joshua to stand together so the twins could
ooh and ahh together at the pretty fairy lights.

Abbey whispered something into Jimmy's ear
and in the next instant the little boy said, 'Fank
you, Daddy.' Becka echoed her brother's senti-
ments and as Abbey glanced at Joshua, she saw
that he appeared rather choked up. It was quite
common for parents to get choked up when their
children did something nice, or sweet, or just

plain gorgeous, but in that one moment Abbey wondered just how many thanks Joshua ever received for all the things he did.

Of course, he had the town rallying around him, helping out, keeping the children safe, but there were also a lot of hours when it was just Joshua and the twins. In the early mornings, when he'd have to get them up and dressed and give them breakfast. Then in the evenings, there would be baths and dinner and bedtime stories.

As they sang 'Happy birthday' to the twins and cut the cake, everyone getting a piece, Abbey watched Joshua more closely, watched the way he interacted with his children. She knew without a doubt that he would do anything for them, even if it meant he got no sleep in order to make sure their birthday was a success. He loved them. Of that there was no dispute, but apart from giving them what they needed, he didn't seem to actually spend time with them. He would wipe their hands when they got sticky. He would take them to the toilet when they danced quickly before him, barely able to hold on. He would pick them up and hold them when they asked him to yet she couldn't help but wonder how often he rolled around with them on the floor, tickling them and laughing with them. Did he love them? Yes. Did he care for them? Yes. Did he know where they were the most ticklish? Abbey wasn't so sure. There was definitely a distance between father and children and she had to wonder why.

The fact that he was trying to put distance between the two of them was painfully evident but it hadn't been completely unexpected. Both of them had been fighting the attraction between them ever since she'd arrived in Yawonnadeere Creek. This morning, alone on her verandah, they'd both lost that fight, giving in to the sensations that had become too powerful to ignore.

Now, though, as people started to say their good-byes, Becka still curled up in her father's arms, Jimmy surprisingly settled in her own, Abbey wondered what was next on the agenda for Joshua and herself. She'd come to the outback to help identify the pieces of her new life, to shuffle them around into some sort of order and hopefully to gain control over them. However, all she seemed to have received on her arrival were more pieces of her life, from way back in her past, mixing with her future. To say she was confused was an understatement.

Soon the pub was back to being just the inner circle, everyone shuffling tiredly around the room, tidying up and setting things back to rights. Joshua was sitting on the other side of the room, Becka sound asleep on his shoulder.

'I'll go put Becka down and then come back for Jimmy,' he told her, but Abbey shook her head.

'I can carry him. No sense in you making two trips. You look utterly exhausted, Joshua. Did you sleep at all?' Abbey stood as she spoke, shifting the deadweight of Jimmy into an easier position for her to carry him.

'I did.'

Abbey rolled her eyes and grinned. 'Sure, but for how long?'

'Long enough to now be utterly exhausted, according to my colleague.' He couldn't help but smile down at Abbey as they called goodnight to their friends before heading next door. Abbey followed Joshua to the rear of the building where they went through the back door and down a small hallway to the children's bedroom. He quickly flicked on their nightlights, which illuminated the room beautifully.

He put Becka into her cot while Abbey did the same with Jimmy, tucking the little boy in before bending down and placing a kiss to his fair head, sliding up the cot-rail to keep him safe throughout the night.

'Your pictures will hang beautifully in here,' Joshua told her, indicating the décor.

'Yes. I had hoped they would.'

'I had no idea you were so good.'

'Just as I had no idea you liked to cook,' she pointed out as they stood in the middle of the room.

He shoved his hands into his jeans pockets

and looked at her. 'Abbey, about what happened earlier this morning…'

'It's fine, Joshua. We don't need to have a post-mortem about it. It was a kiss. That's all. We both had sixteen years of curiosity burning within us and now the curiosity has been satisfied.' She knew she needed to say the words because if she took control of this situation then she should be able to recover from it a lot easier. At least, that was her theory.

'Good. Yes. I'm so glad you feel that way, too.'

'I do. So, we can go back to being colleagues.' Abbey could feel her head begin to pound, part of her wanting him to refute the words she'd said, to drag her back into his arms and plunder her mouth once more. The fact that he hadn't, the fact that he seemed more than happy with her calm, mature attitude, was starting to make her irrational. 'And speaking of that, as I've had far more sleep than you, if you wouldn't mind giving me the phone people use for emergency calls, please? I'll take control of the fort tonight.'

'It's really not necessa—'

'It is, Joshua. Colleagues, remember?'

It was easier to hand over the phone than to stand there and argue with her, especially as he realised she was definitely in stubborn mode. He'd seen her in stubborn mode far too many times in the past and it was ludicrous to even try to argue. Instead, he pulled the phone from the waistband of his jeans and handed it to her.

'Terrific. If I need you I'll wake you but only if it's necessary. The sooner I learn to take control of outback medical emergencies, the more help I can be to you.'

Control. There was that word again. He knew Abbey liked to be in control, to have everything nice and neatly ordered and structured. Being di-agnosed with ovarian cancer and the subsequent treatment must have meant losing all control over her life. That was why she was here. To find her life. That's what she'd told him and if finding control within the bonds of her job were going to help her, who was he to stand in her way? In fact, he could probably learn a thing or two from her, given that he seemed to have very little control where wanting her was concerned. Even as she stood there before him, saying goodnight and thanking him for inviting her to the twins' birthday, he wanted to hold her, to kiss her, to breathe in her sweet, sunshiny scent.

But he didn't. Instead, he said goodnight, watching as she walked from his children's bedroom, emergency phone in hand, leaving him feeling more alone than he'd ever felt before.

CHAPTER EIGHT

NO EMERGENCY happened that night, or for the next two weeks, and after Abbey had been at Yawonnadeere Creek for three weeks, she was having trouble remembering a happier time in her life. Everything seemed to be falling into place. Except for Joshua.

To say that the kiss they'd shared had changed everything was as true as the sky being blue. Now that she knew how it felt to be held in his arms, to feel his body pressed against hers, to have his mouth creating havoc with her equilibrium, all she wanted was more. More touching, more wanting, more kissing.

They'd agreed that the kiss had been a mistake, that their curiosity had been too great to ignore. But now that it was over, it appeared that

Joshua, for one, was more than happy to continue to ignore that incredible tug of desire Abbey seemed to be constantly carrying around with her.

When she was in the pub with their friends or doing a clinic or playing hide and seek with Becka and Jimmy, she was fine. She could be in the same room as him and control her feelings enough so that she didn't throw herself into his arms, even though it was what she desperately wanted.

His touch had awakened something deep within her, something she'd thought had died when she'd entered the operating room to have her reproductive organs removed. Joshua had made her feel like a woman. His tenderness, his powerful need, his gentle caresses. The desire, the passion, the pounding pulse she'd thought she would never feel again had been alive and well when she'd been in his arms. She wanted that feeling again and she knew only Joshua could provide it.

As she stood behind the bar in the Yawonnadeere Creek pub, pulling a beer for one of the locals, Abbey looked across to where Joshua was sitting at a table talking to Mark. His children were sitting on the floor, colouring in.

Her heart-rate increased as she looked at him, the firmness of his broad shoulders, the strong muscles in his back, the smile on his face as he laughed at something Mark had said. Abbey swallowed and sighed as dawning realisation hit her with full force.

She was in love with Joshua Ackles!

'Whoa. I think the glass is full, Doc,' her patron at the bar said.

'What?' Abbey quickly stopped staring at Joshua, looking down at the mess she was making, beer everywhere. 'Oh. Oops. Sorry.' She quickly reached for a clean glass, pulled another beer and handed it over before starting to clean up the mess, she'd made, berating herself for not only being so stupid but for being so obvious in her ogling of Joshua. Then again, it wasn't every day a girl discovered she was in love. She had the right to be shocked by the realisation.

She was startled out of her thoughts by a loud crashing and banging coming from the kitchen. She turned and headed in to see if Dustin was all right. He wasn't. He was reaching for a towel to press to his hand which was now covered in blood.

'What did you do?' Abbey asked as she came forward. There was food all over the kitchen floor, a dropped pan, a few other utensils and the offending knife, which had obviously cut Dustin's hand. The kitchen door opened a second later and Joshua walked in.

'Need help?'

'Yes, please,' she said as she applied pressure to Dustin's hand, forcing him to a stool so he could sit down before he passed out completely.

'Stupid. So stupid of me,' Dustin remarked.

Joshua came over with the first-aid kit and an ice pack. 'Thanks,' she said, accepting the ice pack from him and using it to apply added pressure to the cut. Joshua pulled on a pair of gloves and organised some other bandages while they waited for the bleeding to clot.

'How are you doing there, Dusty? You're looking a little pale,' Joshua remarked.

'Let's get him to the floor,' Abbey suggested, and while she held Dustin's hand, Joshua helped the tall man to sit on the floor, away from the mess.

'Dustin?' Rach came into the kitchen, her eyes widening as she saw her husband and the mess on the floor. 'What happened? Are you all right? Oh, no. Blood.' Rach turned pale at the sight of the few drops of blood that had splattered on the floor with the knife.

'Whatsa madder?' Becka asked as she followed Rach into the kitchen. Her little eyes took in the scene and her cute little bottom lip instantly began to wobble. 'Dusty?' Jimmy was hard on his sister's heels and he, too, was quite distraught at what he saw.

'Dustin's going to be fine,' Abbey soothed the

children. 'Daddy and I are going to look after him per-fect-ly.'

'Rach, can you take the kids out, please?' Joshua said.

'Uh…' Rach was glued to the spot.

'Why don't you both go and draw Dustin a picture? That will help him to feel so much better,' Abbey suggested. 'Take Rach with you. She's very good at colouring in too, remember?'

Becka's lip stopped wobbling at Abbey's words and she slipped her little hand into Rach's. 'Come on, Wach. Let's go make a drawing for Dusty. Come on, Dimmy.' Becka ushered everyone out of the kitchen and Abbey couldn't help but smile at the little girl's forthrightness. It reminded her so much of Joshua.

'A typical bossy female,' Dustin remarked softly.

'Ah, I beg to differ. She likes to take control of things, just like her father.' Abbey grinned across at Joshua, who only frowned in response.

'Right,' Abbey said, deciding it was better to

focus on what they were doing rather than trying to make Joshua smile. 'Let's take a look at it.' She carefully removed the towel and now that the blood had clotted, Joshua began debriding the area.

As she took a closer look at the wound, she shook her head.

'Sorry, Dustin, but it will need stitching.'

'Really?' He didn't seem too happy. 'But that means I won't be able to work in the kitchen for a while. The last time I cut myself I was out of action for three weeks.'

'And we all pitched in and helped,' Joshua said smoothly. 'The same thing will happen again. We look after our own in this town, remember?' He pulled out a plastic packet of sterilised vicryl sutures attached to a surgical needle and another wrapped needle that contained a local anaesthetic.

'A well-stocked kitchen first-aid kit,' she remarked, having mentally planned to take Dustin next door to the surgery.

'As Dustin said, it isn't the first time he's cut himself. After the last time I re-stocked the first-aid kit, to make it easier.'

'Good thinking.'

He handed her the needle and turned Dustin's head away so he couldn't see what she was doing. He knew of old that the young man didn't like injections of any kind. In fact, most of the people he'd come across during his medical career were rather averse to needles.

While they waited for the anaesthetic to take effect, she kept pressure on the wound. Joshua kept monitoring Dustin closely, taking his pulse and getting a blanket to put over him. The last thing they needed was for the tall American to go into shock. When the area around the cut was numb, Abbey asked for the suture. Carefully and with neat precision, she sutured the wound in Dustin's hand closed.

'Would you bandage that for me, please?' she asked Joshua, who merely nodded. She started tidying up, wondering what was wrong with Joshua today. He was quieter, more stand-offish than he'd been in the past few weeks. Had he wanted to take the lead in suturing Dustin's hand? If so, he should have said so. Abbey shook her head, annoyed that she was in love with a man who drove her crazy.

'All done,' Joshua remarked, and she nodded at his expert bandaging. She gave Dustin some painkillers and then together they helped him to his feet, Dustin leaned on Joshua's shoulder as they headed out towards the residence at the rear where Rach and Dustin lived.

The children saw him and began running down the hallway, their pictures in their hands, Rach was hard on their heels. Abbey decided that Joshua could take care of things and returned to the kitchen to start cleaning up.

Joshua joined her soon after, picking up a broom and silently sweeping the area.

'It's fine. I can do it,' she told him. He didn't answer but kept sweeping. 'How's Dustin? All settled?'

'Mark, Giselle, Rach, the twins—they're all fussing over him but, yes, he's settled.' There was a scowl on his face and after another moment of silent sweeping, feeling the annoyance almost steaming from him, Abbey stopped what she was doing and turned to face him.

'What's the problem?' she asked directly.

'There's no problem.'

'There is. You've been as surly as anything today, more so than usual.'

Joshua stopped and leaned on the broom. 'Surly? Me?'

'Yes, you. So whatever it is, get it out in the open so we can deal with it. It's obviously something I've done because you were fine with Mark earlier on.'

Joshua shook his head, peeved that she could read him so easily. It wasn't right. She was supposed to be a woman who had come to town to help out for six months and then she would leave and go on her way, doing whatever she wanted with the rest of her life, and he wouldn't care one iota. Instead, she was Abbey, the girl who had plagued him during medical school, who had come to his town and fitted in so perfectly with his friends and his children. The fact that she could tell when he was out of sorts and that she confronted him on the issue disturbed him way more than he was willing to admit. Miriam hadn't been able to do that, often declaring she had no idea why she'd married him. His own wife hadn't been able to read him yet Abbey could pick up that there was something wrong just by looking at him.

She *knew* him and he realised he couldn't hide from her, the way he'd hidden himself from Miriam. The fact that she looked so gorgeous, with her eyes flashing fire, her chin raised defiantly, her shoulders squared as though she was preparing for battle, only made him ache for her even more. Not many women could look so incredibly beautiful when they were annoyed, but Abbey certainly did. Was that why he'd liked annoying her so much back in medical school?

'Fine.' He exhaled harshly, knowing she also wouldn't drop the subject. When she sank her teeth into something, it was rarely she ever let go. 'My kids like you better than me.'

The look on her face turned from complete stubbornness to one of utter incredulity.

'What? You have to be joking.'

'I'm not.'

'Joshua, those kids *adore* you. You are their sun and their moon. You are their constant in life. You are the one they will always turn to, to kiss their knees when they fall over, to hold close when they cry, to make their world better.'

'But they do what you tell them to, rather than listening to me. I've noticed it since you got into town. First Jimmy and then Becka. They love spending time with you, playing with you, laughing with you.'

'You're jealous,' she said with astonishment.

'What if I am?'

She laughed and shook her head. 'You're a twit.'

'Thank you. I can always rely on you to speak your mind.' He put the broom down and made for the door but Abbey quickly intercepted him, putting her hand on his chest to stop him.

'Stop and listen to what I'm saying.'

He backed away, her brief touch already having sent his desire for her into overload.

'Your children love you, just as you love them, and while you may have been watching me with them, I've also been watching you with them.'

'And?'

'And you need to spend more time *doing* things with them, rather than just *being* there with them. Join in with their silly, crazy games. Lie on the floor and colour in, play chasy with them.'

'Is that why you do it? Is that why you interact with them?' There was a complete vulnerability to his words now and Abbey smiled, pleased she'd managed to get through. 'You are so good with them, Abbey. So natural, so caring, so…' He broke off, watching as she swallowed a few times. It was then he realised she was working hard at controlling her emotions. There may have been a smile on her face but there was sadness in her eyes.

'Oh, Abs. I'm such a cad. Here I am badgering you because I'm jealous of the way my children respond to you when you'll never...' He stopped again and exhaled harshly, noting that his words were making her tear up.

'I'll never be able to have my own children,' she finished for him. 'It's OK, Joshua. We can talk about it. I may have spent the past three years coming to terms with that fact but I also know there are other ways for me to become a parent.'

'Are you thinking of adopting?'

'I can't. Not as a single mother. But I have thought about fostering. Of course, given my work schedule once I leave here and return to the city, that could also pose a problem.' She shrugged. 'I have options. That's something that keeps me going.' She brushed a hand across her eyes, wiping away the tears and pulling herself together.

When she left here. Even hearing her say those words filled his gut with despair. She couldn't leave Yawonnadeere. She fitted in so perfectly and she seemed to be so happy, most of the time… when he wasn't upsetting her.

'I'm sorry, Abbey.'

'I asked you to tell me what was wrong, remember? Can open—worms everywhere.' She smiled, wiggling her fingers, trying to lighten the atmosphere and make a joke of how she was feeling because even just talking about her future, the one she would no doubt spend alone, was something she tried not to dwell on. With the removal of her reproductive organs, with the emotional stress and strain of the situation, Abbey had often ended her days curled in her bed, hugging her pillow close as she cried away the pain. She knew there were ways for her to become a mother and that was great, but deep down inside there was also the emptiness that she wasn't a proper woman any more. The essence of her femininity had been cruelly ripped from her body and now she was just a shell. She appeared whole on the outside but she was hollow within. The biggest problem of all was that she hated herself for feeling this way. She should count herself lucky that she made it.

She was a rational, logical woman. She prided herself on staying in control of her emotions and now, at times like this, when Joshua looked at her as though she were the most incredible woman in the world, like he just wanted to scoop her up and hold her close, protect her, care for her as he did his children, she found it more difficult to cope.

'And I've just swept the floor,' Joshua remarked, watching the emotions flit across her face. Pain, anguish…despair. The need to gather her close, to have her gorgeous body against his was becoming harder to fight with each passing day he spent in her company.

He had hoped that over the past few weeks he'd managed to get himself to a point where he could work alongside her and remain personable but aloof. Now, seeing her like this, all those good intentions went out of the window and floated away with the warm breeze. She was too hard to resist and he put the broom down, intending to go to her, to pull her into his arms, to tell her that he was going to help her make everything better… when the phone at his hip started to ring.

It was the emergency phone and he quickly answered it. 'Dr Ackles.' He listened, then barked out, 'We're on our way.' He snapped the phone shut and replaced it, his mind now in medical mode.

'The helicopter at the rig has just crashed.'

'I'll get Mark and Giselle.' Abbey was instantly in doctor mode and as they gathered what they needed, she couldn't help but admire just how incredibly well they all worked together. A well-oiled team, and it was one she was beginning to realise she didn't want to leave. Not ever.

CHAPTER NINE

AFTER they'd said goodbye to the children, leaving them in Rach's capable care, they all bundled into Joshua's ute, everyone discussing several scenarios, mentally going through the supplies they'd need. Mark called the Royal Flying Doctor Service to let them know of the situation and to have their planes on standby. When they arrived at the rig, the guard already had the boom at the gate up ready for them. The emergency sirens blaring loudly.

Joshua drove them as close as he could to the helicopter landing pad, the wind swirling up around them creating a dust storm.

'Everyone put on safety goggles and masks,' Joshua ordered, and Giselle quickly handed everyone a pair. The wind was fierce and punishing and within a second of stepping from the ute Abbey was already covered in a fine layer of orangy-red dirt. Just as well she hadn't been wearing white today, she thought idly to herself.

Her eyes widened and she blinked, almost in complete disbelief, as she looked at the helicopter, which had tipped over on its side, the rotors all chipped and broken off, pieces of the landing pad and other debris littered here and there.

She followed Joshua to where Pierre was standing, the HOp now back to full health. 'Terry, one of the flight crew, is badly injured,' he said, handing them all fluorescent yellow jackets. 'We've managed to turn the helicopter's engine off and several of the crew are working to get the twenty-odd passengers out. Over there.' He pointed. 'Terry will be the first priority.'

Abbey nodded, grabbing her medical kit close to her chest as she went behind Joshua, one hand on his shoulder in case she lost him in this dust storm. Mark and Giselle had gone over to the helicopter to assist with the evacuation and treat anyone with minor injuries.

Walking over to where Terry lay took longer than she'd anticipated because it felt like the wind was attacking from all sides. Never had she been out in such weather conditions before and she had a new-found respect for the people who lived out here, the dry season often bringing this sort of orange dust storm.

Pierre had organised things most effectively and there seemed to be people absolutely everywhere she looked. He had crews assisting the passengers, crews making sure the helicopter didn't burst into flames. There were people everywhere, making the landing pad look like a busy nest of ants… ants who were all wearing bright yellow jackets to make them more visible.

'Stay close,' Joshua called, taking her hand in his so they could traverse the area, giving support to each other. 'I need you with me, not blown away.' Abbey's heart did a silly little flip at his words even though she knew that wasn't at all how he'd intended them. Of course Joshua only needed her in a medical sense and they continued to pick their way through to Terry. Two other crew members moved out of the way to make room for the doctors.

'Report?' she asked the men loudly, trying to take in what she was seeing. Joshua had the medical kit on the ground and was busy trying to pull on a pair of gloves before getting out some bandages in order to stem the bleeding of the man lying before them.

Abbey remembered Pierre had said the man's name was Terry and it appeared he'd been impaled by a piece of broken rotor from the helicopter. There was a lot of blood and the man was barely conscious. Abbey quickly put her kit down and opened it up, using the shelter of their bodies as best she could to keep things as dust free as possible. Her own hands were already dirty but she still managed to pull on a pair of gloves, not sure they were going to do much good in keeping the dirt away but it was worth a try.

'Terry's not too good,' one of the crew members said. 'We tried to put bandages and stuff around the bleeding but there's just so much of it.'

'OK. We'll take it from here,' she said, and pulled some more heavy-duty packing from her medical kit.

'Severe lacerations to abdomen,' Joshua said, then turned to one of the crew. 'Get Pierre to notify Morgan that we'll need his plane. If we can stabilise Terry and then move him to town, we have a chance of saving him.' He stopped as Terry moaned again.

'Is he allergic to anything?'

'No.' Joshua's answer was immediate and direct and Abbey wondered just how much this man knew of the crew and their medical histories. No doubt, he knew everything. He was that sort of doctor, clear, concise and thorough. 'Past medical history includes an appendectomy and tonsillectomy but that's it.'

'Right.' With fingers that felt quite awkward, Abbey withdrew a vial of morphine and a needle and started drawing up the shot. 'Take these scissors,' she said to one of the crew. 'Cut his trousers away. I need to administer this into his thigh.' She unwrapped a swab while she waited and a moment later she jabbed the needle into Terry's thigh. It took less than a minute for the analgesic to take effect. Terry's features seemed to smooth as the pain was lifted from him.

'Can we get him inside?' She had to lean in close to Joshua to ask the question and almost pulled back when her lips actually brushed against his cheek. She swallowed over her increasing awareness of this man she loved and pushed it firmly away. Now was not the time.

'Pierre will, no doubt, send over a stretcher as soon as possible. Should be here soon,' Joshua had swivelled around so that now he was talking into her ear, his warm breath fanning her neck and not only warming her through but also giving her goose-bumps, which flooded her body with tingles. It was a most bitter-sweet sensation and again one she didn't need right now. 'Now that you've given him something for the pain, we'll get him transferred inside and then keep him as stable as possible while we wait for the airlift.'

Abbey's mind snapped back into doctor mode as she pulled back, looking at Joshua. 'Are you OK to operate?'

'I'll have to be, won't I? Terry needs immediate medical attention.' If Abbey was with him, standing opposite him in the small theatre back in Yawonnadeere, he felt sure that he could cope. When he'd had to operate on Pierre, it had been Abbey who had given him strength and now he was relying on that.

Abbey pulled out another wad of packing and changed the dressing. 'As soon as we pull that piece of rotor out, he'll bleed. Getting him out of this dust is the first step but he'll need saline and plasma.' She started to reconstruct a similar ring-type bandage to the one Joshua had already used in order to pack the wound tightly around the piece of blade still sticking out of

Terry's abdomen. The last thing they needed was for the obstruction to be moving around inside Terry, causing more damage as they shifted their patient.

'Once he's anaesthetised, we need to find the offending arteries and get him stable.' She kept attending to Terry's bandages as she spoke. Without immediate surgical intervention, Terry would indeed die and the last thing Joshua needed was another death plaguing his conscience.

He was about to tell her that he would be OK to operate so long as she stayed with him, that it was important that she accompany him back to their surgery, instead of staying here to help Mark and Giselle. He needed her. As the thought came into his mind, his heart also registered the fact that he not only needed her in Theatre with him, giving him strength, he needed her in his *life*.

He pushed the thought away, focusing on his work. The stretcher arrived and it took five of them to carefully move Terry onto the stretcher and carry it indoors, out of the dust.

'Anything I can do?' Pierre asked, coming alongside Abbey.

'Check with Giselle and Mark and get a report to us on the condition of everyone on that chopper. Tell Mark we need him to anaesthetise so he'll need to come with Joshua and me now. Get any trained first-aid workers out here to assist Giselle with whatever she needs.'

'Consider it done,' Pierre said, and it was then she remembered Joshua telling her that she was now part of Pierre's 'family'. It made her feel less like a locum who was here for six months and more like a part of the team. It was nice.

Once inside and away from the dust, she stripped off the yellow safety jacket as it was too big and had been impeding her movements, leaving it in a heap by the door. Abbey lifted her goggles onto her head and pulled her mask down below her chin, coughing a little.

'How long before Morgan gets here?' she asked Joshua as they performed Terry's observations again.

'Not long.' When Joshua was satisfied, they carried Terry into the corridor to the far door, which was where they were scheduled to meet Morgan. It wouldn't be easy for the pilot to fly in this sort of weather but Joshua assured her that Morgan was the best of the best of the best!

When the plane arrived, they were ready, only waiting on Mark to arrive. Once Terry was transferred and strapped into the small plane, Abbey sat beside him and performed observations again, Joshua looking out into the bleakness in search of Mark.

'Here I am. I'm here,' Mark called, and raced onto the plane, Joshua pulling the steps up as Mark removed his goggles and mask, trying not to spread too much dust around the interior of the plane.

'Let's go,' Joshua instructed Morgan, and soon they were in the air, making the short journey to Yawonnadeere Creek's main street. This time Morgan didn't bother landing at the strip, having arranged for a few of the locals to shift their vehicles out of the way so he could land right on the main road.

'The closer the better,' he murmured, and Abbey had to smile.

In a hospital setting, they would have had the back-up support of being able to call on a surgeon in a particular speciality, to request X-rays, blood samples and anything else that needed to be done. Here, though, it was just the three of them and whilst the situation she now found herself in wasn't an everyday occurrence, the fact of the matter remained—Terry would die without immediate surgery and for that she desperately needed Joshua and his many years of experience and expertise.

When they finally arrived at the surgery, the three of them, with Morgan's help, managed to get the stretcher into the operating bay, transferring Terry onto the operating table. Mark immediately started pulling out the equipment he would need to hook Terry up to a plasma drip, Abbey helping him by getting the IV saline organised on the opposite side. The sooner they could replace Terry's fluids, the better chance the man would have coming through this alive.

With Mark now taking care of Terry, administering the anaesthetic, Abbey turned her attention to Joshua, who had changed into a pair of scrubs and was at the sink, methodically washing his hands. Abbey followed suit and once she was changed, she stood beside him and scrubbed.

'How are you holding up?' she asked.

'If you mean do I keep looking at Terry lying there and seeing Miriam's lifeless body instead, the answer is yes.'

'You can do this, Joshua. I know you can.' Her words were imploring. 'You are a remarkable man and I believe in you. I feel for you, for everything you've been through, but right now you desperately need to find a way to push all of that aside, put it in a box on a shelf in your mind and move forward.'

They continued scrubbing in silence, Abbey hoping Joshua would listen to her words and push aside the traumatic circumstances that had stopped him from operating in the first place. She knew he was capable of great things, she'd known that sixteen years ago in medical school, but now that she was in love with him she wanted him to have as much faith in himself as she had in him.

'And if he dies?' Joshua asked as they pulled on gowns and gloves.

Abbey took a deep breath and slowly let it out, meeting his gaze. 'Then he dies and you and I will grieve together. Then we'll move on. It's the way of the world.'

Finally, they were ready and standing next to their patient, ready to do whatever they could in order to save his life. Mark had managed to cut away Terry's clothes and to prepare him for surgery.

'Thanks for getting him ready, Mark,' she said as she looked down at their patient, then met Joshua's gaze. 'Ready?'

He was quiet, not saying a word, but Abbey

waited. She could almost see his internal struggle and she silently cheered him on, willing him to realise that he *could* do this. He was a strong man who had become lost in the face of tragedy…but he was still a strong man.

'What do we do first?' she asked, and this time received a reply.

Joshua slowly exhaled into his mask then put his hand out. 'You hand me the scalpel.'

Elation shot through Abbey and the smile beneath her mask was bright and encouraging but she damped down her emotions, knowing she needed to focus. She picked up the scalpel from the tray and placed it firmly into his outstretched hand.

From then on Joshua was focused, issuing instructions so Abbey knew exactly what he needed and when. Usually this sort of operation would require more staff, given that instruments needed to be changed and the wound packed because the instant Joshua removed the obstruction from

Terry's abdomen, things had to move much faster.

Still, between the two of them they managed. Mark worked wonders with the anaesthetic and kept a very close eye on the IV bags.

'Pass me the locking forceps. I think I've got the last one,' Joshua said, and Abbey did as she was asked. When he'd clamped the offending artery, she suctioned the area to ensure it was clear but a moment later blood was still pooling.

'There's another one and we've missed it.' Joshua shook his head and started a methodical search.

'Changing the plasma bag again,' Mark told them. 'Guys, we only have two left.'

'It's OK, Mark. Joshua can do it. He'll find that artery.' Her words were firm and without question.

Joshua kept working but his gaze locked with Abbey's for a moment. 'You believe in me that much?'

'I do.' Again, there was no hesitation in her tone.

'Right. Let's do this.'

It wasn't too long before he'd found that final ruptured artery and clamped it off. After another hour they were ready to insert the drains Terry would need. Abbey watched as Joshua continued to operate with steady hands and a clear head. After another hour Terry's wound was stapled closed and Mark was starting to reverse the anaesthetic.

Joshua stepped back from the table and looked at his handiwork. Abbey watched him closely, unsure what was going to happen next, but he simply nodded once before turning and walking over to the bin.

She followed suit, stripping off her gown and gloves, disposing of them in the correct bins before walking back to the sink to wash her hands. She couldn't believe the bubbling excitement she felt towards Joshua. He'd overcome his own fears. He'd pushed past his block of being unable to operate. He'd told her that every time he thought about operating, every time he stood next to a table, all he saw was his wife's limp, lifeless body lying there.

Today, however, he'd pushed through everything and he'd saved Terry's life. Their patient would be facing a long, drawn-out recovery but he would live. Abbey turned round, wanting to talk to Joshua, but saw he'd left the room. She headed to the consulting rooms and found him on the phone, no doubt talking to the RFDS.

She shifted from foot to foot, waiting for him to finish his calls. What had just happened, the breakthrough he'd made, was an event that needed to be celebrated. He needed to be aware that he'd just achieved an amazing feat.

When he finally replaced the receiver, he looked over at her, still staying seated behind his desk.

'That was Pierre. Giselle seems to have taken control of the situation out at the rig, and the wind has died right down so the dust is starting to settle.'

'And the patients?'

'Mostly whiplash injuries, cuts from the glass. Two people who she thinks might have minor concussion but apart from that, everyone's been very lucky. The RFDS are on their way to pick up Terry and everyone else can be either flown to Adelaide on Morgan's plane or wait until tomorrow to return home.' His words were deep and filled with satisfaction.

'All's well that ends well?'

He nodded. 'It could have been a lot worse.'

'Agreed.'

'Terry?'

'Stable. How about we check on him, then head next door to see your children and have a nice cool drink?'

'Sounds good.' Joshua stood and came around the desk. As proud of him as she was, it was clear he was having difficulty dealing with what he'd just accomplished. He held out his hand to her and she immediately took it. 'I couldn't have done that without you.'

'I think you would have managed just fine,' she said, secretly pleased with his words but unable to take the credit. 'You're quite a man, Joshua Ackles.'

'And you are quite a woman, Abbey Bateman,' he said, and tugged her into his arms. As there was no place on earth she'd rather be, she went willingly, her arms sliding past his waist and up his firm back. Abbey's eyes closed in delight as she relaxed against him, holding him just as close, wanting to reassure him that she was there for him.

She rested her head against his chest, the sounds of his heart beating its steady lub-dub filling her with happiness. His scent wound its way around her, filling her senses, and after a few breaths she sighed, feeling the stress of her own day melt away. Abbey felt a little guilty because she was supposed to be there for Joshua, to be support- ing him, helping him, and yet with his warm arms around her, holding her close to his gorgeous body, it was *her* tension that seemed to be dissipating rather than his.

They stood there for quite some time, neither one talking, content just to let the silence reign. He had no idea what sort of perfume she was wearing but it wasn't overpowering and neither was it pretentious—just like Abbey herself. He liked to watch the way she moved, gracefully, with poise and purpose. He was so aware of her presence, no matter where they were, in clinic, at the pub, working in an emergency, and in every situation he seemed to want her more and more.

Being aware of another woman in a physical, sexual capacity was wrong. He was destined to be alone, that much he'd realised after Miriam's death. Now, right here, standing in his private haven with such an incredible woman in his arms, Joshua wasn't so sure. His life had changed after his wife's death and now it was changing again with the arrival of Abbey in his life.

She might downgrade the role she'd played in Theatre but he'd stood there, looking down at that operating table, Terry's anaesthetised body desperate for medical intervention, and all he'd seen had been Miriam's lifeless body lying there. He'd wanted to pull back, to turn away from the situation, to get as far away from that room as possible, the stress, the memories, the pressure all assailing him.

Then he'd heard Abbey's soothing words. And looked into her mesmerising eyes. He'd seen the strength and belief she had in him. It was because of Abbey that he'd been able to hold out his hand and request the scalpel. It was because of Abbey that Terry was now alive and would, in time, make a full recovery. It was because of Abbey that he was now starting to see past the pain and terror that had plagued him in the past and look forward to a happier future.

He'd been astounded at his reaction to Abbey, at the way she made him feel whenever she looked at him. There was hope in her eyes, hope for him. He angled back slightly and looked into those brown depths of hers and when she met his gaze, he could *feel* the faith she had in him. He had no idea what he'd done to deserve such trust but it was there and he felt it with a certainty he hadn't experienced in a long time. Having someone believe in you was a powerful feeling and it was because of Abbey and Abbey alone that he'd been able to break down the barriers that had been binding him.

She felt so perfect in his arms and he was so grateful she was allowing him to hold her. It was as though she was giving him an energy transfer, recharging him, and he had to admit the sensation was like an aphrodisiac. The least he could do was to thank her.

'Abbey.' As he spoke her name he felt her loosen her hold but he didn't want her to go anywhere. He wanted to keep her close, to have her scent wash around him, to have her strength seeping into him so that he could continue his journey forward. 'No. Stay, please?'

Abbey's answer was to link her arms around his body again and snuggle into him. The action was almost his undoing and the urge to press his mouth to hers, to sample the softness he knew she'd offer was becoming increasingly harder to fight. Now that he knew how incredible she tasted, how perfectly his mouth seemed to fit with hers, how delighted he was to hold her close to his heart, it seemed almost pointless to fight it.

He wanted Abbey. He'd always wanted Abbey, he realised with a start. Long before he'd met and married Miriam, he'd wanted Abbey. Acknowledging this fact to himself helped him to say what he needed to say. She was a very special woman, dear to his heart, and she deserved to be treated in a special way.

'Abbey,' he started again, then stopped and cleared his throat, a little surprised to hear his own voice filled with desire. 'I just wanted to thank you for today.'

Abbey sighed and shifted her gorgeous body against his, her voice relaxed when she spoke. 'You are most welcome, Joshua.'

Joshua closed his eyes, trying to focus on his

words rather than the way the woman in his arms was making him feel. He wondered if she understood the degree to which she'd helped. It was now becoming imperative that she comprehend how dear she was to him, how important her opinion was to him, how attracted he was to her. 'You don't understand, Abbey. I never thought I'd ever be able to operate again without going through the trauma of the past.'

'I know,' she murmured, her voice vibrating through his chest. The sensation only magnified the powerful need he had for her. 'I could see the struggle inside you.'

'Really?'

She smiled and tightened her arms around him, gently caressing the muscles of his back through the cotton scrubs he still wore. 'I know you, remember.'

'People change.'

'Sometimes they do but you haven't, not in essentials. You were always honest, trustworthy, hard-working and focused. We were very similar, probably why we argued so much.' She chuckled a little at her words and the sound reverberated through him, filling him with delight.

Joshua smiled at her as though he was unable to believe he was allowed to hold her so close. He was also coming to realise that the sensations he was feeling weren't just lust or desire. It was more than that. He wanted Abbey, of that there was no doubt, but it wasn't temporary want, it was permanent.

Ordinarily, that should have scared him but for some strange reason it didn't. He looked down into her upturned face, seeing the glow of happiness, the glow of belief, the glow of pride in him flow through her. 'You are one very special lady,' he murmured, and then, as though he was unable to restrain himself any longer, Joshua bent and brushed his lips across hers. It was the briefest of kisses and he'd initially intended it to be just a way of saying thank you but the instant they touched, everything around them changed.

The room seemed to melt away, the problems

of the world disappeared, there was only the two of them, standing there, arms entwined, faces alive with wonderment at the energetic aware-ness passing through both of them.

All rational thought had fled from his mind the instant he'd brushed his lips over hers. Now all he was aware of was Abbey and how incredible she was making him feel. He didn't deserve it. He didn't deserve it at all.

'Abbey. You are so beautiful.'

His words came out in a rush, his breath fan-ning her face, his words causing her heart to pound even more fiercely against her chest. It wasn't the first time he'd called her that but she would never grow tired of hearing him say it. Given that she had so much pain, that she didn't feel like a whole woman any more, hearing him call her beautiful gave her hope. Hope that one day, maybe with Joshua's help, she might feel more 'normal', more like a true woman.

'I can't stop thinking about you and it's starting

to drive me crazy,' he ground out, his voice filled with repressed desire.

'I know…the feeling.' Abbey's breathing was still increasing, becoming more erratic with each passing moment they stood there in each other's arms, intent on looking deeply into each other's eyes. 'I think about you all the time.'

'You do?' He cupped her cheek with one hand, his warmth flooding through her.

'I dream about you every night, wanting to be in your arms again, wanting to feel your lips against mine.'

'Really?'

'Oh, yes,' she breathed. Her words, mixed with the desire he saw in her eyes, was enough for him to bury his face in her neck, nuzzling the skin, pressing kisses to her sweet, soft flesh. Abbey angled her head, granting him further access, pleased her hair was still pulled back in a pony-tail from their impromptu operating session.

He worked his way back towards her mouth, taking his sweet, tantalising time. 'I've wanted to kiss you, to touch you like this, for so long, Abbey. You taste like…'

Abbey waited, hypnotised by his words, by his touch. Never had a man spoken to her like this before. Joshua made her feel so cherished, so special, so feminine. The way he was feathering her neck and cheeks with kisses, the way one hand slid into her hair, freeing her brunette locks from the clips that still bound them, allowing the silky tresses to bounce around her face. The way his other arm was gathering her closer, drawing their bodies together… Everything about him was making her light-headed with passionate pleasure…and she wanted more.

'Sugar and spice.'

A small smile twitched at her lips at his words.

'And all things very, very nice,' he breathed as he pulled back just a smidgen to look into her eyes. It was as though he was seeking her permission, to be able to take the next step without fear of repercussions, and Abbey's answer was to slide her hands up his firm, muscled back, loving the feel of his body beneath her fingers.

She arched towards him, urging him to close the gap between them. 'Kiss me, Joshua. Please?'

Even though she'd said the words, even though he'd felt the reaction of her body against his, it was only in that moment that he realised Abbey wanted him every bit as much as he wanted her.

As though finally sure, as though realising this kiss would definitely mean more, that the stakes had been raised, that she was becoming way too important in his life, Joshua did as she'd asked and put his mouth firmly on hers.

Both of them sighed into the embrace, holding tight as the eagerness, the need to explore spread over both of them. She half expected the kisses to be hot and heavy, as they'd been last time, but he surprised her yet again by starting off slowly, not wanting to rush but rather to explore. He was a surgeon and he knew the advantages of being thorough in explorations.

Her taste combined with her glorious scent was a heady combination and one he knew he was fast becoming addicted to. When he opened his mouth to deepen the kiss, she came with him for the ride, matching him in intensity as slowly they began to explore further.

He had no idea where this might take him, where it might lead them, what the future held for either of them, but at the moment nothing mattered other than being with Abbey, and for the first time in a very long time Joshua started to get a sense of belonging. Holding Abbey, being with her, was enough to rock his world and in a blinding flash he realised he couldn't imagine his life without her in it.

As his mouth worshiped hers, he started to wonder just how he could keep Abbey here in Yawonnadeere Creek when her six-month locum came to an end.

CHAPTER TEN

FOR the next week, Abbey wasn't sure exactly what was happening between her and Joshua but it was definitely an improvement on where they'd been before their last kiss.

As though following an unspoken rule, both of them weren't flaunting their intense attraction to each other but neither were they hiding it. Little touches here and there, looks shared across a crowded pub, eating lunch at the bar. All of these things weren't out of the ordinary as far as everyone else in the town was concerned but for the two of them it was definitely new.

It was as though they both needed to get used to moving out of their comfort zones, taking that scary step forward from the lives they'd wrapped themselves in as protective shields. Change was never easy but Abbey knew that coming here, being a part of this town, loving Joshua as she did was a change she was willing to accept. The scary part was trying to figure out just how Joshua felt about her.

He hadn't made any effort to kiss her again, even when they'd been alone after finishing their clinics the other day, but he was more than happy to sit with her over a cup of herbal tea, to just talk and get to know her better.

He would put a hand on her shoulder and give it a little squeeze whenever he said goodbye of an evening. He would lean closer to say something near her ear, his breath floating over her neck causing goose bumps to break out down her spine.

The other big change he'd made to his life was to spend more quality time with his children, just as Abbey had suggested. Just yesterday, they'd all been lying on the floor in the back room at the pub, colouring in and sharing pencils. Spending more time with Becka and Jimmy had also freed up a bit of time for Rach to continue looking after her husband, whose hand was heeling nicely.

Every night when Abbey went to sleep, she would stand at the window in her front room, looking over at Joshua's house, the twinkle fairy lights still strung beautifully around the front, the twins demanding the lights stay. It *did* look as though another world was just beyond those eaves, another world where Joshua and his children lived, children who had become as much a part of her heart as their father.

Abbey would blow three kisses towards the house, one for each occupant, and then she'd head to her bedroom, lying beneath the ceiling fan, dreaming of a time when she might also be included in the gorgeous family who made her feel so incredibly happy.

This is it, she realised on Monday morning, one month after arriving in the outback. You've found your new life. She jiggled a teabag in the cup and took a sip, surprised to realise her search was over. She loved Joshua, she loved the twins and she desperately wanted to be a part of their lives.

Would they let her merge? Let their lives intermingle? She knew the twins wouldn't mind but would Joshua? Would he be able to trust himself enough to enter the world of marriage once more, especially as his previous marriage hadn't been one built on a solid foundation? They'd talked a lot over the past week and he'd admitted to her that his relationship with Miriam hadn't been all that strong, that Miriam had baulked at having children but had only given in because he'd insisted.

'I've realised, quite recently, that even if she hadn't died, we wouldn't have made it. Our marriage would have ended in divorce and I would still be here in Yawonnadeere, raising the twins on my own.' It had been a sobering admission but with it he could move his life forward—at least, that's what Abbey was secretly hoping—and she wanted him to move it forward with her by his side.

'Abbey?'

She was startled from her reverie at the sound of Joshua's voice, calling loudly to her. She quickly put the cup down and hurried to the front of her house.

'Abbey?' Joshua was standing on his own verandah, holding open the front door to the surgery. A car was out front with a concerned mother weeping on Giselle's shoulder. Mark carried a boy of about eight through the open surgery door.

'What is it?' she asked, rushing across the road, both of them heading in after Mark.

'Eight-year-old boy having an asthma attack,' he explained.

Abbey frowned and shook her head. 'Third one in the past two days. Put him in my clinic room, Mark. I'm all set up.'

The distraught mother was coming in the door, calling for her son. Giselle could be heard trying to keep the mother back and out of the way.

'Arthur? Arthur? Is he all right? Is he…?' She covered her mouth with her hands as she saw her son sitting up on the examination couch, Abbey fitting an oxygen mask over the boy's face as Joshua adjusted the cylinder for the correct dose. The boy rasped the air in.

'He's going to be all right, Janice,' Joshua soothed. 'Go with Giselle and let us look after him.'

'Bronchodilator,' Abbey was saying, Joshua and Mark helping her.

'Set oxygen saturations to ninety-five per cent.'

'Deep breaths for me, Arthur.'

'Pass me that stethoscope.'

'That's it. Nice and deep. Good boy.'

'We'll get you all sorted, Arthur.'

'That's it. Nice deep breaths.'

Between the three of them, it didn't take too long to calm the boy down and soon he was re-united with his mother.

'You did the right thing, bringing him in when you did,' Joshua said.

'I nearly sent him to school this morning. He

was coughing through the night but with all the dust we've had around lately, I didn't think anything of it. Then he started making these gasping, choking noises and…' She shook her head again, her hands starting to tremble.

'You did the right thing,' Joshua reiterated, knowing they needed to keep the mother calm so the son also remained calm. As a parent, it hadn't taken him long to realise that children could easily pick up on an adult's emotions and that was enough sometimes to set them off at an unhappy tangent.

He glanced across at Abbey. Could she pick up on his emotions? The ones that were saying he didn't want her to leave Yawonnadeere in five months' time? That he wanted her to stay here as his medical partner? To be a part of his life?

He had no idea how to tell her what he was feeling, mainly because he wasn't quite sure himself just what he felt for Abbey. The fact that the emotions were very different from the ones he'd felt for Miriam were a given, but after one bad marriage caution was now his friend. Besides, he had the twins to consider. Would making Abbey a permanent part of their lives be good for them?

The fact that the little mischievous three-year-olds needed a mother was also true and they certainly adored Abbey. Abbey, in turn, adored his twins and he could see, just by watching them all together, how incredible she would be as a mother.

Although they'd started being more open with each other, the one part of his life Joshua had kept off limits was his house. Apart from the evening of the twins' birthday, when she had carried Jimmy inside and put him into his cot, he hadn't invited Abbey over.

It had been a strategic move because he could picture her all too clearly in his house, in his life, in his arms. Change wasn't an easy thing for him to accept or deal with but the thought of Abbey leaving, of him enduring his life without her in it, was starting to become an unacceptable scenario.

As he watched her monitoring Arthur, soothing Janice and making arrangements for Mark to monitor Arthur overnight, Joshua decided that tonight would be the night. He'd ask Abbey to come over for dinner, to see just how well she fitted into his home. His heart pounded at the enormous step forward he was taking but he knew that sometimes you had to be brave and bold to get what you wanted.

After she'd finished writing up the medical notes, she looked up and smiled at him and it was all he could do not to close the distance between them and haul her back into his arms. In fact, it was becoming more and more difficult to keep his distance but he was determined to take things more slowly this time around, to make absolutely sure he wasn't making a mistake. If he could have Abbey in his life and keep his heart safe at the same time, he might finally stand a chance at being happy.

The rest of the day seemed to tick by very slowly. Joshua tried a few times to ask her over for dinner that night but each time something cropped up to stop him. For a change, the day had been rather busy, plenty of people needing medical attention, and it wasn't until they were in the pub, enjoying a relaxing glass of wine, that Joshua had his opportunity.

'You would think I'd know this menu off by heart,' Abbey said, smiling at him over the top of the piece of laminated paper. 'Still, I can't seem to decide what I'd like for dinner tonight.'

'Uh…about that.'

'Yes?' She put the menu down and looked at him, sipping her drink.

'Well, would you like to join me for something to eat?'

'Sure. You don't usually eat here on a Monday night. In fact…' she glanced at her watch. '…isn't it past the twins' bedtime?'

'I didn't mean eat here, Abbey. I'm asking you over for dinner.'

'Oh.' Her eyes widened in surprise while inside she was jumping up and down like an excited three-year-old. She hadn't pushed Joshua at all, wanting him to take his time before he asked her over but to say she'd been getting impatient for it to happen was an understatement. 'Can I help you get the kids ready for bed?'

Joshua smiled. 'Why do you think I'm asking you? Those two are like streakers after their baths. I just get one wrestled to the floor when the other starts. They can both climb out of their cots, so I just leave the sides down now.' He shook his head. 'It's as though since they've turned three, all of the rules have changed, except no one told me.'

Abbey laughed as she picked up her hat. 'Oh, poor old dad.'

'Hey, enough of the old,' he remarked as the twins chose that moment to run over to him. Seizing the opportunity, he picked one up in each arm and stood. 'Time to go home, monkeys.'

'No,' they both chorused together.

'Abbey's coming with us,' he added.

'To my house?' Becka was completely surprised.

'To my house?' Jimmy repeated.

'Yes and yes,' Joshua said, placing kisses on the tips of their noses. Thanks to Abbey, his relationship with his children couldn't be better, despite the rules having been changed. He now made sure that every day, even if it was an extra cuddle at night or a game of hide and seek before starting his morning, he spent quality time with his children.

'Let's go,' Abbey said, holding out her hands to Jimmy who went willingly into her arms. That night, they trooped out of the pub looking very much like a family and Abbey's hopes started to rise once more. This was a good thing, right?

'She's definitely a daddy's girl,' Abbey remarked as she started running the bath. Little Becka was resting her head on her father's shoulder, her arms firmly around his neck.

'You think?' Joshua's own hands were protective as he held his daughter, relishing the affection she was giving him. 'Or am I a girl's daddy?'

Abbey laughed. 'Either way, the two of you are adorable together. Hold onto her while I get Jimmy.' The little boy was currently running up and down the hallway, going from one end of the house to the other, laughing and stomping on the wooden floorboards as he went. He was certainly a fast runner but Abbey didn't think he was any match for her.

'Good luck with that,' Joshua said as he took Becka into the bathroom, getting her ready.

'Where does he get all his energy?' Abbey called up the corridor.

'Well, he gets to have an afternoon sleep, has all his meals prepared for him, has all his laundry done for him and spends most of his time playing and not caring about anyone else in the world but himself.'

Abbey laughed at this answer. 'Oh, if only life were that simple for the rest of us.' Then she headed off to catch the little boy.

Joshua undressed Becka, making sure her pretty curls were tied up off her shoulders and out of the way before putting her into the warm bath, kneeling down beside her as she started to play with her toys.

Becka splashed the bathwater and laughed, her blue eyes bright with delight as her father reacted.

'Hey. No splashing, missy.' Joshua quickly rolled up his sleeves and tickled her tummy. 'You are a cheeky monkey, aren't you?'

Becka giggled and splashed again. 'Daddy wet.'

Her laughter, her words, her big sparkling eyes reiterated just how much he loved her and just how much she needed a mother. He turned at a sound in the doorway and saw Abbey walking in with a wriggling, naked Jimmy wrapped up in a towel.

He instantly stood. 'Come here, matey.' He took the squirming boy from Abbey and plonked him in the bath next to his sister. It took only a second for the two to settle down and start playing to-gether—friends for ever they would be, such was the bond between the twins.

As he stood there, watching his children inter-acting, a lump rose in his throat. Abbey was standing beside him and it seemed the most nat-ural thing in the world to slip his arm about her shoulders. She didn't shy away from the contact, closing her eyes and committing this moment, these sensations of warmth and contentment to memory.

'Abbey?' His voice was deep, his tone intent, and as she looked at him, her heartbeat tripled in a matter of seconds. He took one of her hands in his free one and raised it to his lips, brushing a feather-light kiss across her knuckles. 'Thanks for coming tonight.'

Abbey's mouth went dry at his touch, at his caress, at the kisses he was pressing to her hand. Slowly, she uncurled her fingers and tenderly touched his cheek, loving the fact that he was allowing this. 'Thank you for asking me,' she returned.

'I've wanted to ask you for some time now but—'

'Shh.' She put a finger to his lips. 'You don't have to explain anything to me.'

As he looked down into her face, her saw that her eyes were conveying just how much she'd wanted to be this close to him again. He turned her slightly so that she was facing him, his arms slipping around her waist, urging her a little closer. She stepped forward and slid her hand around his neck, the warmth of his skin causing her own to tingle with excited anticipation. The look in his eyes was the same as before, deep and dark with repressed desire. He wanted her, of that there was no doubt. He wanted to kiss her and the way his gaze flicked from her eyes to her parted lips and back again only added fuel to the fire that was burning within her.

'I love your neck,' he murmured, dipping his head and pressing his lips to her carotid pulse.

'So I've gathered,' she replied, her hands sliding into his hair. She'd been unable to stop dreaming about him, to stop craving him, to stop loving him.

'What does this mean?' she whispered in his ear.

'I don't know.'

'Joshua?'

'I can't stop thinking about you. I've tried, Abbey. I've really tried but I can't.' He rubbed his hands up and down her back. 'I want to spend time with you, to hold you, to touch you. I want to kiss you over and over again. There's a powerful attraction between us, Abbey, and I've never felt anything like it before. I want to understand why I'm feeling this way, why I need you so much.' His words were intense, gut wrenching and almost pleading.

'It's as though this…thing between us has just risen up and slapped us both in the face,' she agreed.

She felt him smile before he lifted his head and

look down into her smiling face. 'You have a way with words, lady. I like that about you. You're open, you're honest and you speak the truth from your heart.'

'Are you sleepy, Daddy?' Jimmy wanted to know, and it was then that both adults seemed to realise where they were. Joshua looked at his son.

'A little bit sleepy, mate.' With great reluctance, he let Abbey go, both adults feeling a bit self-conscious being caught out by a couple of three-year-olds.

'I want to west my head on Abbey's shoulder, too,' Jimmy said, and then yawned as if to prove his point. 'I'm sleepy, too.'

'I know you're sleepy, matey, which is why we need to get you clean, get you fed and get you into bed.'

'I'll go see if I can find the twins' pyjamas.' She walked out of the bathroom and into the children's bedroom and it took her a moment to realise that something had changed since she'd last been in there.

It was then she saw them. Framed on the wall, above the children's cots, were the pictures she'd drawn them for their birthday. Joshua had put them up, giving them pride of place. A lump formed in Abbey's throat as she realised a part of her would always be with the twins, no matter what happened between her and their father.

Every time they met, every time they were together, every time he looked into her eyes, all she wanted was to rush forward into his arms, close her eyes and rest her head. She needed someone to hold her, to comfort her, to be there for her, and she wanted that someone to be Joshua.

She was tired and she'd been through so much of her own personal trauma. She was working hard at coping with her bleak future. She knew she had a gift for caring, for being there to help others. She was a giver and she always had been. Her positive attitude had served her well throughout her trials and tribulations but there were times when she had no energy, when she felt like giving up, when she needed someone else to care for her.

Yes, she desperately wanted that person to be Joshua and she wanted it so badly because she was in love with him. She'd fallen in love with a man who was incredibly handsome, incredibly strong and incredibly generous with his time and energies. She loved it when he held her, when he kissed her, when he looked deeply into her eyes as though she was the only woman in the world who mattered to him.

She held up a little pink nightie, complete with flowers and butterflies, and couldn't help closing her eyes and snuggling it against her face. The fresh scent of laundry detergent filled her senses and she imagined giving little Becka a cuddle while she was wearing the nightie, of tucking the moppet into her cot and dropping a kiss to her forehead.

Then she imagined kissing little Jimmy good-night before tiptoeing out of the room, to sit down with their father, his strong arms coming around her, making her feel cherished and loved and incredibly special. They would be together. The four of them. A family.

'Abbey?'

She heard Joshua's voice from the bathroom and opened her eyes, brushing away the tears she'd been unaware had fallen. 'Stupid cancer,' she murmured, damping down the anger she often felt towards the disease that had ravaged her body, leaving her feeling less of a woman. She knew it was stupid to feel that way but that's how it was. That's how it had been for the past few years, until she'd bumped into Joshua again. He made her feel wonderful and special. He made her feel…whole and that was a sensation she wanted to have for the rest of her life.

'Can you bring me another towel, please?'

Pulling herself together, Abbey reached for a tissue and quickly blew her nose before gathering the children's nightclothes together and then heading to the linen cupboard where she extracted another fluffy white towel. When she re-entered the bathroom, it was to find the floor rather wet, the two children in the bath with decidedly less bathwater than previously and Joshua, standing straight, almost drowned with splashed water, a goofy grin on his lips.

'Your towel, Daddy.'

He grinned at her as he rubbed his arms and then his hair, leaving it messy and a little bit spiky. It only made him even more drop-dead sexy and Abbey swallowed over the urge to run her fingers through those gorgeous locks of his, to help him take off his wet clothes and rub the rest of him dry. Good heavens, he was like sex on legs and she was having a difficult time controlling her reaction to him.

'Oh, honey. Don't go looking at me like that,' he growled. 'Not when we have an audience.' His voice was deep and husky as though he knew exactly how he was affecting her, and in return it was causing a chain reaction to explode within him.

'Let's get the kids out, fed and into bed,' he said again, forcing himself to turn away from the alluring Abbey and get Becka's towel ready.

'Yes. Of course. We need to focus on the children.' Abbey was speaking softly and more to herself but when Joshua began to chuckle, his rumbling laughter washing over her as though it were the most wonderful sound in the world, she realised he'd heard her. 'Sorry,' she mumbled.

'Hey,' he said as he lifted Becka from the bath and wrapped her up. 'Don't be sorry, Abbey. I like the way you look at me.'

Abbey swallowed. 'You do?'

'You'd better believe it.'

'Jimmy's turn,' the toddler demanded, and stood up in the bath. Abbey was quick to take him out before he slipped over and placed him on the bathmat, wrapping him in his fluffy towel. 'I love you, Abbey.' He leaned into her and her arms naturally came about his little body, picking him up and cuddling him close.

'Oh, sweetie. I love you, too.' She dropped a kiss

to his head and then looked from son to father, Joshua's eyes smiling with delight.

'My son has good taste.'

She followed him into the twins' room, trying not to dwell on that last comment of Joshua's. They dressed the children for bed, the twins talking with animation about the pictures she'd drawn for them.

'They both look at those pictures every night and say "Goodnight, Abbey" before they go to sleep,' Joshua told her. 'You've won them over.'

Abbey tried to swallow over the lump in her throat. 'They've won me over, too.' Sucking in a deep breath, she clapped her hands together. 'What's next on the list?'

'Dinner,' the twins chorused, and ran out to the kitchen, leaving the adults to follow.

Abbey sat in Joshua's kitchen, having helped the children to set the table, and watched as he whipped up a healthy meal of chicken and vegetables.

'I keep forgetting how you do amazing things

with food,' Abbey remarked as she ate, not realising she was hungry until the mouth-watering aromas had filled the air. It was an odd setting, sitting around a dining table, eating with Joshua and two children, in a house she didn't live in, feeling as though everything was right with her world.

Both children chattered through dinner, keeping the conversation flowing on the importance of red versus green crayons and which one really was the best. Becka, though, seemed to be struggling to stay awake and Abbey's heart turned over with love and laughter as she watched the little girl's head nod every now and then, her spoon clattering to her almost empty plate.

'Poor baby,' she murmured, and quickly took her out of her high-chair. Becka snuggled into her. Abbey breathed in deeply, the scent of the child filling her heart with love. Dropping a kiss to the moppet's head, she met Joshua's gaze.

'Seems as though it's unanimous.'

'What is?'

'We all like our Abbey.'

'Oh.' She wasn't sure what to say to that and so decided not to say anything else.

'I'll go put Becka in her cot.'

'Right. I'll help Jimmy finish his dinner.' He picked up Jimmy's spoon and started feeding his son. Jimmy was more than happy to have the responsibility of feeding himself taken over by someone else as he, too, seemed to be tiring more and more with each passing second. 'See you in a few minutes.'

Abbey held Becka in her arms, rocking her back and forth, ensuring the child really was asleep before putting her down in her cot. Joshua came in as she was tucking Becka in and when Jimmy started to cry, protesting about being put to bed even though he was almost half-asleep already, Abbey started to sing a soothing lullaby.

The strange sound, the sweetness of it and the fact that he was almost out of energy to fight any more, had Jimmy settling down quite quickly and thankfully not waking his sister. With the nightlight on, Abbey and Joshua tiptoed out of the room.

'Abbey, you have a beautiful voice.' Joshua's words were intent and heartfelt as they headed into the kitchen. He switched the kettle on, taking out two mugs and then pulling out a small box of herbal teas. 'Chamomile?' he asked, and she nodded. 'I should have expected it.'

'What?'

'That a beautiful woman should also have a beautiful voice.' He turned to look at her as he spoke and Abbey tried not to blush under his close scrutiny.

'Thank you.'

'You were wonderful with the children,' he commented, sitting opposite her as he waited for the kettle to boil.

'So were you. Joshua, you are a good father. Trust in that and trust your instincts.'

He nodded. 'You're right. You always are.'

'It's clear that your children love you as much as you love them.'

'Strange that it's taken me three years to realise that.' He laughed without humour. 'I've always loved them, always provided for them, been there for them when they needed me, but it was you who showed me that I hadn't taken the time to get to *know* them, to find out who they are as individuals. I'm really enjoying it.'

He reached across the table and took her hands in his. 'I feel as though I'm constantly thanking you, Abbey, but, really, you have made a big difference in my life. You've helped me to face up to my past with Miriam, to realise that my marriage wasn't that strong and that I was bound to end up a single parent. Sure, it's devastating that Miriam had to die and I still feel a level of responsibility for her death, I always will, but I've also been able to let a lot of those past hurts and guilt go and I couldn't have done that without you.'

'Stop. You're going to make me blush,' she said, trying to joke her way through it. Joshua rubbed his thumbs over her knuckles, caressing her skin, causing her heart rate to increase. He was far too alluring and when he touched her, especially as tenderly as he was now, she found it difficult to think or remember anything.

'Abbey. Ever since I've met you, way back in medical school, we've had this bond, this strange, often antagonistic but powerful bond. It's linked us, helped us, guided us and brought us to where we are. Here and now.'

'Spanning sixteen years.'

'Exactly.'

Abbey swallowed, listening intently to what he was saying, trying to guess where it might be heading and trying to focus as his rich, deep tones washed over her, turning her mind to mush.

'We get along really well and there's no denying there's a definite attraction between us. You know about my past, you've met my children and they adore you.'

'What are you saying?' she asked, a little bewildered.

'I'm saying that you belong with us.'

'Us?' Abbey's eyebrows hit her hairline.

'Me. The children.'

'Belong?' Abbey was totally confused now.

'I think we should get married.'

CHAPTER ELEVEN

ABBEY paced around her house, unable to sleep, unable to make any rational sense out of what had happened that evening.

'I think we should get married.'

Joshua's words resounded through her mind again and again. It made no sense. Well, she rationalised, the way he'd laid everything out so neatly, so clearly, so concisely had made perfect sense, but the fact that he'd put no emotion into his so-called proposal meant that it made no sense at all. Not really.

'It makes perfect sense,' Joshua had said, letting go of her hands to finish making their cups of tea. 'Watching us all tonight, you can see that we're good together. My kids don't have a mother and I'm not trying to be callous or unkind but the fact of the matter is that you are perfect motherhood material. Abbey, the way you relate to them is amazing. You'd be so wonderful for them.'

'And that way I get to be a mother without having children of my own.' Abbey had said the words Joshua had been alluding to.

'You're so natural. You were meant to be a mother.'

'Thank you.' Abbey had stood, ignoring the tea on the table, needing some distance from him, not wanting him to touch her again because she couldn't think properly when he did that. Right now it was imperative that she think properly.

'Obviously, I'm moving too fast.'

'Just a little, Joshua. Asking…what you're asking, well, it's a little…'

'I know. I understand that you might want to take some time to think it over.'

'I think *you* should take some time to think this over. Just because I can't have children and your children need a mother is no reason for you to start proposing marriage.'

'Abbey.' Joshua walked over and placed his hands on her shoulders. 'What is it?'

'What is it?' she repeated with utter incredulity, remembering to try and keep her voice down so she didn't wake the children. 'Are there any other reasons why you think we should get married? Or is convenience the only one that comes to mind?'

'Well...of course there's the attraction we feel for each other. I like you, Abbey. I like you a lot and I know you feel the same about me. It's been building for...well, since med school.'

'Like?' Abbey whispered the word in disbelief. Like? He thought she just *liked* him? It would have been so easy to say yes, especially as she loved him with all her heart, but she couldn't enter into a marriage with a man who didn't love her. She already had an emptiness deep inside her body, she didn't need another one deep inside her heart.

'Listen, take some time,' he said. 'You don't have to give me an answer right away.'

'But are you sure, Joshua? Are you sure this is what you really want?' Abbey met his gaze, her eyes intent and waiting…waiting for him to say the words that could change her life, the words that could make this situation turn from one of a garish nightmare to one of joyous sunshine. Every woman wanted the man of her dreams to propose, to confess his undying love, to sweep her off her feet in a silly romantic gesture, but apparently, in her case, the man of her dreams appeared to be more practical than romantic.

Abbey continued to pace around her house, still unable to focus on anything other than her churning thoughts. Around and around they went but the one they kept stopping on was the memory of Joshua's face when she'd turned down his proposal.

'I don't need time to think about it, Joshua.' She'd seen hope flare in his eyes but she wasn't looking for hope—she was looking for love. She may have found it with him but it was obvious that he hadn't found it with her. He *liked* her and maybe that's what his first marriage had been based upon—like. It didn't matter what had happened between Joshua and his first wife, it didn't matter how their marriage had worked or functioned. She was Abbey, she was a romantic at heart, and she was a woman who believed marriage between two people should be grounded in love.

'I'm afraid I have to decline your generous offer.'

'But, Abbey. It'll work. We're compatible. All four of us. We fit.'

Abbey had picked up her hat and taken a few more steps towards the door. 'No, Joshua. Obviously we don't.'

He'd stood there about to make another convincing argument but she didn't want to hear it. She *couldn't* hear him go on and on about 'like', about fitting neatly together, about being compatible, when all she wanted was to hear him tell her that he loved her. The fact that he didn't showed her he was either incapable of loving her or that he hadn't thought this whole thing through as thoroughly as he usually did. He'd been married to another woman and had lost her in such tragic circumstances. Perhaps because of that, he'd decided the next time he'd marry using his head rather than his heart.

Whatever his reasons, the real reasons, it didn't matter. His reasons for proposing weren't compatible with her own and that was all there was to it. She would live out the rest of her life, always being in love with him and never being able to have him. It was just another bitter twist to her future and one she had to learn to live with.

Reaching for the phone, she dialled her friend Eden. Perhaps it would be best for her to take a job working somewhere else, anywhere else, to get away from the outback. She would have to figure out a way to work with him for the next five months but after that she had to leave. Anywhere was fine so long as it was away from Yawonnadeere Creek and the people she loved so much.

* * *

Joshua had tried calling Abbey several times after what had happened on Monday night but she was either very busy or she was simply ignoring him. On Tuesday, after settling the children with Rach, Joshua headed out to the rig, leaving Abbey to deal with any patients on her own. She was more than capable, she knew the routine and Pierre had asked last week for a meeting. Now seemed as good a time as any.

'You're in a bad mood today,' Pierre said as he watched Joshua pace around the small office. 'What's wrong?'

'Wrong? What makes you think anything's wrong?'

'I know you, mate. It's very rare that you're out of sorts like this.'

'Bad mood. Out of sorts. You really know how to make a guy feel good.'

'Who's been making you feel otherwise?' Pierre asked, and when Joshua didn't respond, he ventured, 'It's not that lovely Abbey, is it?'

Joshua stopped pacing and spread his arms wide. 'She turned me down.'

'Did you offer her a permanent job? Because if you did, that's a smart move. She belongs out here.'

'How can you tell whether or not a person belongs?' he growled, not wanting to talk about Abbey but at the same time wanting to talk about nothing else.

Pierre sat back in his chair and pondered for a moment. 'There are several reasons why people come to the outback. Most come for a job, which is the case for the majority of people living in and around Yawonnadeere Creek.'

'I came here for a job and I stayed.'

'You stayed because you were lost,' Pierre pointed out calmly. 'Being isolated can either destroy a person or it can enhance them, and the only way you know which way you're going to go is by facing your fears. Believe me, I speak from experience. Years ago, something…unsavoury happened to me and I hid myself away in

Coober Pedy, of all places. I took to the bottle, the missus almost left me—I was a mess.'

'Really?' Joshua was surprised. He'd known Pierre had a past but he'd never asked.

'Too right, mate.'

'What happened?'

'I faced my problems, head on. Stopped drinking, turned my life around and look where I am today. I'm a changed man. My wife's still with me and my kids are growing up proud of their dad instead of being embarrassed by him. That's worth everything, in my book.'

'I love my job here. My kids are happy and my world seemed just fine before Abbey came.'

'You were broken, mate. You had been through such a tragedy, losing your wife. But then in waltzes that gorgeous Abbey, bringing a tube of superglue with her.' Pierre laughed at his own joke. 'She's sorted you out good and proper. Don't be letting that one go, mate.'

'I've had to.' There was pain and hurt in Joshua's tone and he wondered how long it was going to take to recover from losing Abbey. He couldn't hide it, not from his friend.

'What? Why? You fool.'

'Fool?'

'She's good for you. You're good for her. She needs to be loved. You can see it in her eyes. I don't know what she's been through but there's something there and she needs you just as much as you need her.'

Joshua clenched his jaw. 'I asked her to marry me and she said no.'

'Did you ask properly? Romantic, like? Get down on one knee? Tell her how much you love her? How much you can't live without her? Girls like that stuff. I tell you, even after almost thirty years of being married to my missus, she still likes a spot of romance.'

Joshua was silent and as he looked out the window, the sky seemed to clear, the clouds opening as the sunlight appeared to shine down. 'Romance?'

'Oh, for Pete's sake, boy. At least tell me you told her you loved her, right?'

'Love? I don't…' Joshua stopped, unable to deny the emotion, realisation dawning but with a loud resounding thump on his heart. 'I. Love. Abbey.' The words were spoken in utter amazement. 'I love Abbey,' he breathed, and in that one split second his world made sense once more.

'Of course you do, you twit. Any fool could see that just by looking at the two of you together. Go and fix things with Abbey, son.'

'But…she said no. She doesn't want me.'

'Sure she does.'

'I don't know how to fix this.'

'Sure you do. Believe in yourself. Believe in her. Now, get out of here. We can discuss rig business another day.'

Joshua was out of the door before Pierre had finished his sentence. On the drive back to Yawonnadeere, he thought back over everything Abbey had said the other night when she'd declined his offer of marriage. He thought about the way he felt when he touched her, when he held her, when he kissed her, and couldn't believe his stupidity at not realising that he had been in *love*. He thought about the way he'd felt, watching her with his children, his heart swelling with love at the way she seemed to light up when Jimmy had put his arms about her. Abbey was meant to be a mother, there was no doubt about that, but she hadn't wanted to be a mother without love from the father.

'I love Abbey.' He whispered the words out loud, then laughed as he realised just how right they sounded. 'I love Abbey,' he yelled to his car, and as there were no speed limits out here, he put his foot down. He had some romancing to do.

Joshua's heart was beating wildly in his chest as he raised a hand to knock on her door. He checked his bow-tie was straight and brushed a hand down the lapels of his dinner jacket. He knew he was about to make an absolute fool of himself but he didn't care. He needed Abbey in his life and if that required him to break out of his comfort zone to win her back, that's exactly what he would do.

Rapping his knuckles on the wooden door, he waited, fidgeting with his tuxedo jacket, brushing fluff from his trousers and tapping the top of the white box he'd placed on the step beside him. He picked up the single red rose and waited. Everything was in place. He was ready.

Abbey didn't come to the door.

Joshua frowned and checked his watch. It was almost seven o'clock. He'd left the kids with Rach and Dustin, the twins excited to be having a sleepover at the pub. He wanted to be free this night, to let happen whatever was going to happen, and all because he loved Abbey.

Why wasn't she answering the door?

Concern began to flood him and this time he knocked louder. Where was she? Was she all right? Had something happened to her? He clenched his jaw as he imagined her lying on the carpet after tripping over and accidentally knocking herself out on the coffee table. He knocked again, his agitation increasing as a few different scenarios played out in his mind.

Automatically, his hand went to the doorknob and although he found it unlocked, he didn't want to go in. He needed her to come to the door so he could be all romantic and make this night a special one for her.

He knocked again, this time more like an insistent pounding, his impatience to know she was all right rising with alarming speed. She was *his* Abbey and he wanted to protect her, no, he *needed* to protect her, and that was why he'd come here tonight, why he'd organised such an elaborate romantic evening. So he could win her back, to show her and to tell her just how much he loved her. But if she didn't open the door soon, she was in danger of having him forgo all his planning just so he could get to her. She was *his* Abbey.

He was raising his hand to knock yet again, the mental pictures of Abbey in complete distress flicking through his mind one after the other.

She could be hurt. She could be unconscious. She could be bleeding.

When the door was finally wrenched open, she stood there in a bath robe, her hair wrapped in a towel.

Or she could have been in the bath.

'Joshua?' Abbey glared up at him, her hands on her hips. 'What are you doing? I thought someone had been murdered out here with the insistent way you were pounding on my door.'

'Hmm.' This was not the way Joshua had thought the evening would begin. 'No. Uh…no accident, no murder, just me…being impatient.' And worried, he added silently.

Abbey frowned, giving him a steady appraisal, taking in the tuxedo. 'Going to a function? It's like thirty degrees.'

'Huh? Function?' It was then he realised he was still holding the rose in his hand. 'Uh…sort of. This is for you.' He thrust the rose out towards her.

'For me? Joshua? What's going on?'

He shrugged then sucked in a deep breath before exhaling it slowly. 'I missed you.'

'You missed me? You only saw me this morning. Briefly, I might add, but you still saw me.'

'I still missed you.' His words were heartfelt and insistent and Abbey's heart started to flutter. 'And I also wanted to say that I'm sorry.'

Abbey took the rose and brought it to her lips, breathing in its sweet but subtle scent. Joshua watched her, their eyes locking, and he hoped, he prayed, he wasn't too late, that he was able to undo the damage he'd caused yesterday evening.

'You're so beautiful,' he murmured, and Abbey self-consciously fingered the lapels of her towelling robe.

'Well…er…thank you. Um…would you like to come in?' She still held the rose near her lips, the smooth velvet touch sweet and seductive.

'Thank you.' He stooped to pick up a large white box and came into her house.

'I'll just go and change.' She smiled nervously, her brain finally clicking in to recall that she was naked beneath the robe. She blushed a little at the thought.

'Here.' He held out the box. 'This is for you.'

Abbey took the box. 'What is it?'

'A dress.'

She stared at him. 'You bought me a dress?'

'I did. I'm madly hoping I guessed your size correctly.'

'How? There are no designer shops in Yawonnadeere.'

'I am a man of many talents, Dr Bateman.' He tapped the side of his nose and she decided to simply go along with whatever it was he was doing. The last thing she'd expected tonight was to find the man of her dreams standing on her doorstep, wearing a tuxedo, giving her a rose and then buying her a dress! What was next?

'OK, then.' She smiled brightly at him, accepting the box, thankful the rose stem had no thorns as she juggled the two. 'I guess I'll go and change.'

Joshua paced around her living room, noting

the changes she'd made to old Dr Turner's residence since she'd arrived. There were quite a few photos and pictures on the walls as well as some dried wild flowers. The old weatherboard house seemed quite different from when Dr Turner had lived here and he knew it was simply Abbey's ability to make it her own that made it now so heart warming.

He looked at the paintings, mainly watercolours but all of them very good. Most were scenic paintings and then he looked closer at one of them when he recognised the view of the main street in Yawonnadeere as seen from Abbey's verandah. Then he looked at the next one and found it was of his home, covered in twinkle lights.

'Joshua.'

At the sound of his name, he turned slowly, his eyes still drawn to the painting. 'Your artwork is astounding, Abbey. You really are quite—' He stopped, almost swallowing his tongue as his gaze drank in the sight of Abbey in the long, snug-fitting red dress he'd bought for her. 'Abbey.'

Her name was a caress on his lips and her stomach churned with knots of anticipatory delight. She had no idea what was going on but she liked it. Whatever was happening now most definitely had something to do with his apathetic proposal of marriage, she was sure, and as he obviously had something planned, she wasn't going to spoil it.

She'd had next to no time to get ready with an impatient Joshua prowling around her living room, but Abbey had opened the box and gaped with delight at the most glorious dress she'd ever seen. Scarlet, strapless and seductive, she'd slid the smooth fabric over her head and been astonished that it fitted her to perfection. In fact, there was very little that was left to the imagination.

Quickly applying some mascara, blush and a bit of lipstick, she'd twisted her hair around and clipped it up off her nape, leaving a few loose tendrils. She'd smiled seductively at her reflection, knowing how much Joshua liked to nuzzle her neck and hoping she would drive him completely insane by tempting him all night long.

She clipped on the diamond circle pendant she always wore, a gift from her parents because she'd survived ovarian cancer, and found it enhanced the dress to perfection. Black strappy sandals were all she had for her feet and she was pleased that she'd decided to pamper herself tonight with a pedicure and a bubble bath.

'It fits,' she remarked, sliding a hand down her hip.

'I can see that.' Joshua nodded, his mouth dry as he stared at the woman before him. 'I know I've called you beautiful before, Abbey, but…' He took a few steps towards her. 'You're exquisite.'

Her smile brightened, her eyes alive with happiness. 'Thank you.'

He cocked his arm towards her. 'Shall we?'

Abbey slid her hand nervously around his elbow. 'I gather it isn't worth my while asking where we might be going?'

'You are correct, even though it shouldn't take

you too many guesses, given the lack of five-star restaurants in town.' He pulled the door closed after them. He was definitely Mr Attentive tonight.

'We're not going too far,' he murmured, and then proceeded to walk her across the road to his house.

'We're here already? You weren't kidding when you said we weren't going far.' She raised an eyebrow and laughed as they walked down the corridor, past their consulting rooms, past the little operating theatre, stopping at the door that led to his living quarters.

'This is all…' Abbey laughed, smoothing her hand down the gorgeous dress. 'It's so amazing. Thank you.'

'You haven't seen half of what I have planned.'

'I don't need to,' she said, and placed her hand on his arm. 'It's just wonderful that you're here, with me, doing this…whatever this turns out to be.'

'Ahh, so you *are* a romantic at heart.' He took

her hand in his and raised it to his lips. 'There's still so much I don't know about you, Abbey.'

'And I you.'

Joshua let go of her arm to unlock the connecting door between surgery and house. It was kept locked to ensure the twins didn't accidentally get into any part of the surgery. 'Close your eyes,' he whispered, his hand on the doorknob.

'What? Why?'

'Shh.' He put a finger across her lips and then, as though he was unable to resist, brushed his mouth across hers. 'All shall soon be revealed.'

Abbey dutifully closed her eyes, allowing him to lead her through the door, loving the feel of his body so close to hers. She kept hoping this wasn't a dream, that she wasn't about to wake up and find that she was all alone in her house, crying herself to sleep yet again. She'd had so many sleepless nights from cancer, from worry, from sadness, but lately her sleepless nights had been because of Joshua.

The man she loved had proposed to her but

he hadn't proposed because he loved her. Now, though, here she was, in a gorgeous dress, being led by Joshua into his home, her eyes closed as she carefully felt her way forward, the high-heeled sandals she wore feeling foreign on her feet after weeks of flat shoes.

Once they were through the door, he stopped and re-locked the door and she admired him for his diligence. She had no idea where the twins were and given the level of silence in the house, she wondered whether they weren't perhaps next door at the pub with Rach and Dustin.

'Ready?' he asked, close to her ear.

'Yes. Can I open my eyes?'

'You may.' Joshua stood and held his breath, hoping she liked what he'd prepared.

Abbey gasped with awe and wonderment as she walked into the house. It was obvious right from the start that she'd guessed correctly with regard to the twins. They were most definitely not here. Joshua had gone all out, turning the *inside* of his home into a magical fairyland. The entire entryway, living room and dining room had been decorated with tiny tea candles, making the room glitter and glow so beautifully, it literally took her breath away. Dried rose petals were on the floor, their scent encompassing and welcoming her.

Joshua smiled at the way she kept opening and closing her mouth like a fish, pleased he'd managed to stun her. 'And now, if you'd like to come this way...' He led her to a meticulously laid table, set for two. It was then Abbey realised there was a delicious aroma in the air and turned to look at Joshua.

'You've cooked me dinner?'

He took her hands in his as they stood, surveying the room. 'It was either this or the pub,' he joked, then immediately sobered. 'I wanted tonight to be special. I can't do that, can't do right by you, in a rowdy room full of people.'

'I presume the twins are with Rach and Dustin?'

'Having a fantastic time, excited to the hilt with their special sleepover at the pub. Giselle and

Mark were going to make them a special dinner of noodles and cheese—'

'Their favourite,' she interjected.

'And then Rach and Dustin were going to turn their spare room into a tent complete with cardboard stars, covered in aluminium foil to make them shine and sparkle when they hang them from the roof.'

'I don't think the twins are going to want to come home after that.' Abbey bit her lips as she took in what he was saying. 'So, everyone knows we're here, together?'

'They do.'

'And you're all right with that?'

'I am.'

'Are you? Joshua.' Abbey let go of his hand and caressed his cheek. 'This is so strange, so different. Lovely, but it's not really you.'

'Yes, it is.' His words were vehement. 'Tonight, I am more *me* than I have been in a very long time and I'm this way because of *you*.'

'Me?'

'Abbey.' He stopped, pulling out a chair and urging her to sit. 'When Miriam died, a part of me died, too. I know, it's natural. We were married, we were connected. The fact that I blamed myself for her death was…well, it was what I did. Since then I've tried to piece my life together, trying to make it fit again, and it wasn't until you told me that the pieces of my life have changed that I realised you were right. My life had changed, dramatically, and it changed even more when you came back into it.'

'Me?' she said.

'Abbey, the pieces, the strange puzzle pieces of my life, are almost back together, fitting in different ways, but there's one piece, one very important piece, that's missing. That's you, Abbey. I need you in my life.'

'You do?'

'Abbey, you've opened me up. You've talked to me, you've seen right through to my heart. You're such a caring, giving, wonderful woman and I love you for it.'

278   THE DOCTOR'S DOUBLE TROUBLE

'You…you…?' Her eyes widened at his words and her mouth dropped open when he went down on bended knee, gathering her hands into his once more.

'Love you? Yes. Most passionately. You have helped me to face some of the toughest fears I've ever had and I've gathered strength from you. Last night, when I asked you to marry me, I hadn't realised then exactly how I truly felt about you. I saw you with my children, witnessed just how much they loved you and I just wanted to give you the opportunity to always have such a love surround you. You deserve it. You're a wonderful woman and you'll be an incredible mother. All I was really sure of last night was that I needed to have you near me, near us. The thought of you leaving me at the end of your six months here has been keeping me up at night. I had to find a way to keep you here, keep you close, although it wasn't until earlier today that the penny finally dropped why.'

He stopped and brought her hands to his lips,

kissing them again. 'You've been through so much, my darling Abbey. I could tell, when you were with the twins, just how much being a mother really means to you. But it could have been so much worse. If they hadn't found your cancer in time, it could have taken your life.' Tears welled in his eyes as he spoke the words. 'And that…that would have been a real tragedy.

'You are special, my beautiful, wonderful Abigail. You have a precious gift of giving and despite what you've faced, what emptiness you may carry around inside you, you continue to give to others. You gave to me…you've helped to make me whole again. Now, please, let me give to you. Let me give my love to you and let me share the love of my children. My life, without you, is meaningless. Sure, if you don't feel the same way, I will go on. You've taught me how to do that, how to not close myself off from those who care about me. You've shown me that my children need me very much and for those things alone I will be forever grateful but please, *please*,

tell me that I'm not too late. Tell me that you fee
the same way about me as I feel about you?'

'Joshua.' Abbey swallowed over the lump in
her throat, the tears in her eyes spilling over and
dropping from her lashes to her cheeks. Joshua
stood, tenderly scooping her into his arms and
kissing away her tears.

'Abigail Bateman, I love you and I hope, with
all my heart, that you will agree to marry me
to be by my side as together we raise those two
gorgeous children who need us. Please, Abbey
Be my wife?'

'Joshua.' Abbey sucked in a few breaths, unable
to speak due to the choked emotions he'd evoked
with his eloquent words.

'Say yes,' he urged.

'Yes.' The word was whispered and it was all
she was able to get out before he brought his
mouth to hers, sealing their love with a powerful, all-consuming kiss. 'I love you, Joshua,' she
finally said after many more glorious kisses. 'I
have for quite some time but I simply couldn'

allow myself to accept your proposal the other day knowing you didn't feel the same way.'

'I was a fool.'

'A fool for love.' She kissed him back. 'Thank you for loving me and for giving me the one precious gift I could never give you—a family.'

'It's about time someone gave to you, Abbey and I'm honoured to be that person. I promise to give you my love, for ever.'

'For ever,' she sighed, and allowed herself to be gathered close into his arms as they sealed their love with another heart-searing kiss.

EPILOGUE

'I'M VERY excited, Mummy,' Becka told Abbey as they sat at a table in the Yawonnadeere Creek pub.

'*I'm* excited, too,' Jimmy added. 'She always gets in first. I'm always about to say something and then Becka goes and says it first. It's not fair.'

Abbey laughed. 'That's enough you two, now finish off your special milkshakes because it's time to get you both home and into bed.'

'Aww, Mummy,' they complained in unison. 'Do we have to?'

'Yes,' their father said, coming up behind Abbey, a papoose over his shoulder as he patted the six-month-old baby inside that he'd finally managed to get to sleep. 'Listen to your mother.'

Joshua bent down and pressed a kiss to his wife's lips.

'Is he asleep?' she asked, peering around the inside of the baby sling.

'He is asleep. Now we've just got to get these two monkeys to bed and we could settle in for a quiet evening together.' He waggled his eyebrows up and down suggestively and Abbey couldn't help but blush.

'I can't believe it,' Giselle remarked, coming over and clearing the plates from their table. 'You have been married almost one year and he can still make you blush.'

'You'd better believe it.' Joshua kissed his wife again and patted the baby held close to his heart. He hadn't believed he had the love inside him to shower on another child but little Charles, cradled within, had proven him wrong. One of Abbey's friends who worked closely with PMA in Tarparnii, had helped them arrange the adoption of Charles who had been left an orphan two weeks after his birth.

Now, he was part of their family, the twins taking on even greater responsibility with a young baby to care for.

'I can't believe we're going to be *four*, tomorrow.' Jimmy clapped his hands with utter glee.

'The sooner you get to sleep, the sooner you can wake up and be four years old,' Joshua encouraged, trying to get them out of the place so he could go home and spend some time with Abbey. He'd always known she would make the most wonderful mother and he hadn't been wrong. To see the way she loved and cared for all three of their children was incredible. She had so much to give and in giving, she received so much in return.

'And you'll decorate the house like a magical fairyland again, won't you, Daddy?' Becka asked as they waved good-bye to everyone in the pub.

'Twinkle lights again? It feels like only yesterday you actually let me take them down,' he protested. 'Aren't you a little old for a magical fairyland?'

'Daddy! Bite your tongue.'

'Fairylands are special, Dad,' Jimmy pointed out matter-of-factly.

Joshua looked longingly at Abbey. 'Looks as though we'll have to wait a little longer before having our special time together.'

'We can get the kids off to bed and then hang the lights together,' she whispered close to his ear. 'You can wear just your denim jeans, like you did last year but this time I'll get to touch your body, explore those contours and—'

'Fine. We'll hang the lights,' he told his daughter, his wife laughing happily as they headed into the house.

Abbey organised for the twins to brush their teeth and then settled them in their beds, their room now decorated differently from twelve months ago. This was now more of a pre-schooler's room, with drawings and paintings, some done by Abbey, some done by the twins, hanging around the room.

As she kissed her children good-night, Abbey's

heart turned over with love for them. How powerfully she did love her family, the recent addition of Charles being the icing on their already overflowing cake.

Once the twins were settled, she went into Charles' room and looked at him in his cot, bending down to kiss him sweetly on the head. 'Goodnight, my son. Mummy loves you very much.'

'Hey there,' Joshua said from behind her and she turned, her smile wide as she saw her husband, dressed only in his old denim jeans, posing in the doorway. 'Ready to light up my world, Mrs Ackles?'

Abbey chuckled and slowly walked towards him. Thanks to Joshua, she no longer felt incomplete. He and their children had filled the void in her life, making her the happiest woman in the world.

'Lead the way, sexy man, and I'll be forever following.'

MEDICAL™

Large Print

Titles for the next six months...

March

DATING THE MILLIONAIRE DOCTOR	Marion Lennox
ALESSANDRO AND THE CHEERY NANNY	Amy Andrews
VALENTINO'S PREGNANCY BOMBSHELL	Amy Andrews
A KNIGHT FOR NURSE HART	Laura Iding
A NURSE TO TAME THE PLAYBOY	Maggie Kingsley
VILLAGE MIDWIFE, BLUSHING BRIDE	Gill Sanderson

April

BACHELOR OF THE BABY WARD	Meredith Webber
FAIRYTALE ON THE CHILDREN'S WARD	Meredith Webber
PLAYBOY UNDER THE MISTLETOE	Joanna Neil
OFFICER, SURGEON...GENTLEMAN!	Janice Lynn
MIDWIFE IN THE FAMILY WAY	Fiona McArthur
THEIR MARRIAGE MIRACLE	Sue MacKay

May

DR ZINETTI'S SNOWKISSED BRIDE	Sarah Morgan
THE CHRISTMAS BABY BUMP	Lynne Marshall
CHRISTMAS IN BLUEBELL COVE	Abigail Gordon
THE VILLAGE NURSE'S HAPPY-EVER-AFTER	Abigail Gordon
THE MOST MAGICAL GIFT OF ALL	Fiona Lowe
CHRISTMAS MIRACLE: A FAMILY	Dianne Drake

MILLS & BOON™

MEDICAL™

Large Print

June

ST PIRAN'S: THE WEDDING OF THE YEAR	Caroline Anderson
ST PIRAN'S: RESCUING PREGNANT CINDERELLA	Carol Marinelli
A CHRISTMAS KNIGHT	Kate Hardy
THE NURSE WHO SAVED CHRISTMAS	Janice Lynn
THE MIDWIFE'S CHRISTMAS MIRACLE	Jennifer Taylor
THE DOCTOR'S SOCIETY SWEETHEART	Lucy Clark

July

SHEIKH, CHILDREN'S DOCTOR...HUSBAND	Meredith Webber
SIX-WEEK MARRIAGE MIRACLE	Jessica Matthews
RESCUED BY THE DREAMY DOC	Amy Andrews
NAVY OFFICER TO FAMILY MAN	Emily Forbes
ST PIRAN'S: ITALIAN SURGEON, FORBIDDEN BRIDE	Margaret McDonagh
THE BABY WHO STOLE THE DOCTOR'S HEART	Dianne Drake

August

CEDAR BLUFF'S MOST ELIGIBLE BACHELOR	Laura Iding
DOCTOR: DIAMOND IN THE ROUGH	Lucy Clark
BECOMING DR BELLINI'S BRIDE	Joanna Neil
MIDWIFE, MOTHER...ITALIAN'S WIFE	Fiona McArthur
ST PIRAN'S: DAREDEVIL, DOCTOR...DAD!	Anne Fraser
SINGLE DAD'S TRIPLE TROUBLE	Fiona Lowe